MW01129792

THE VATICAN'S FINAL SECRET

BY

FRANCIS JOSEPH SMITH

Copyright by Francis Joseph Smith

All rights reserved. No part of this book may be reproduced, stored in a retrieval system, or transmitted in any form by any means without the prior written permission of the publisher, except by a reviewer who may quote brief passages in a review to be printed in a newspaper, magazine, journal, or on-line.

First Printing

This is a work of fiction. Names, characters, businesses, organizations, places, events, and incidents either are in the author's imagination. Any resemblance to actual persons, living or dead, events, or locales is entirely coincidental.

The Cataloging-in-Publication Data is on file at the Library of Congress.

PUBLISHED BY AMAZON

www.amazon.com

Printed in the United States of America

Also by FRANCIS JOSEPH SMITH:

The Devil's Suitcase

The Vatican's Last Secret

(James Dieter Book 1)

The Vatican's Deadly Secret

(James Dieter Book 2)

DEDICATED TO MY FAMILY.

FACTS:

There once existed a golden room bedecked in floor-to-ceiling amber, gold, and semiprecious stones.

It positively glowed.

Two different kings called it their own, and it graced multiple palaces, ultimately becoming the prized treasure of the Russian nobility.

In 1941 the Nazis invaded, and the 180-square-foot Amber Room—today worth anywhere from $200 million to ½ a billion—vanished without a trace. Making an entire bejeweled room that has often been called *the eighth wonder of the world*, disappear.

The Amber Rooms origin began over 300 years ago when the newly minted King of Prussia, Frederick I, commissioned a new work of art for his Charlottenberg Palace. He called on sculptor Andreas Schlüter to design a room made almost entirely out of amber. The orange, yellow, and red hues of amber were set into gold leaf to make panels of intricate mosaics that were finished off with other semiprecious stones. The mosaics took eight years to complete and were installed in 1709.

Its stay in Prussia did not last very long. In 1716, the second King of Prussia, Frederick William I, who allegedly prized his military prowess over the artistic endeavors honored by his father, gifted the room to Peter the Great of Russia as a symbol of peace between the two countries *and a sign of their alliance against Sweden.*

The Russians treasured their gift. The amber mosaics were installed in the Winter House in St. Petersburg until 1755, when Czarina Elizabeth moved the panels to the Catherine Palace.

There, it was a favorite spot of the royal family, who loved to entertain their noble guests surrounded by the warmth of the gleaming walls.

Because the Amber Room occupied a bigger space in the Catherine Palace than in its previous homes, the Russians brought in a trove of amber to enlarge their masterpiece to 180 square feet and over six tons of amber stones.

And there it sat in the Catherine Palace for over 80 years, until WWII.

In 1941, the Nazis invaded the Soviet Union. As with their other conquests, they immediately set their sights on looting the nation's treasures. In particular, Hitler wanted the famed Amber Room.

The Soviets tried to protect the Amber Room first by taking it apart and moving it. When that failed (the amber started crumbling and it was deemed too dangerous to continue), they tried to hide it in plain sight by wallpapering over the ornate walls.

However, the Nazis weren't fooled. They quickly found what they were looking for, disassembled it, packed it into 25 crates, and shipped it back to Königsberg, Prussia, where the room was reassembled and put on display in the Königsberg castle museum under the watchful eye of noted amber expert—Dr. Alfred Rohde.

This was the Amber Rooms last known location; the trail of the lost masterpiece goes dark from here. There are several theories about what may have happened to the precious mosaic walls. Some think they were destroyed when Allied bombers targeted the city in 1944.

Others say Rohde was ordered to pack up the panels when it became clear the war wouldn't go on much longer.

Most think Rohde put them on a train that has yet to be found, while others think it was on a ship that sunk to the bottom of the ocean.

To this day, Russia still believes Germany has concealed the panels of the fabled Amber Room in a secret location only known by a select few.

As with most art mysteries—including those involving the countless works pillaged by the Nazis that have never been found—Governments and treasure hunters have continued in their search for the Amber Room, and will continue to do so, until the mystery of its disappearance has been solved once and for all.

And that day is today.

CHAPTER 1

September 7, 1941 - Puskin, USSR

The Catherine Palace had stood majestically since 1710 when Peter the Great presented the palaces estate to his beautiful young wife, Catherine. Over the years, the palaces ornate, baroque design was enlarged to almost 740 –meters in length. A massive structure by any definition. Like many structures in the small town of Puskin, the Catherine Palace painted radiantly in a brilliant robin's egg blue, trimmed in white, and gilded with over 200 pounds of gold.

Up until the Russian revolution of 1917, Catherine Palace had served as the imperial family's summer residence. Filled with 18th-century paintings and ornate rooms, the palace surrounded by a 1,400-acre park complete with fountains, bridges, the Agate Pavilion bathhouse and the Great Pond.

It was often referred to as a Russian version of Versailles along with its sister palace, Peterhof, located 24 kilometers north in Petersburg.

However, the Catherine Palace had a room like no other palace in existence. Located deep within the structure was a space that Catherine had tended to call her *Special Room*. A room so special that Kings and Queens from all over Europe would flock in the summer months eager to visit and sit in its splendor.

The *Special Room* was also known as the Amber Room.

It had also caught the attention of Nazi Germanys Adolf Hitler. He had placed the room's acquisition at the top of his list. Only he was not going to buy it; *he was going to steal it.* Since his troops invaded the Soviet Union in June 1941, they had steadily fought their way across its eastern territories.

Now they stood at the gates of Leningrad, Stalingrad, and Moscow.

****

ANATOLY POPOV, the director of the Catherine Palace, barked out orders to his paltry workforce of eight men and two women; the hundreds of others who worked in the Palace Museum had already been conscripted into a local militia to save Leningrad. However, urgency hung in the air. For the past week, as German forces moved into the Pushkin area, just 24 kilometers south of Leningrad, he and his workers had attempted to disassemble and move the Amber Room to safety. Without the proper tools, the dry amber began to crumble. Anatoly immediately halted the work. They would have to devise some other way to remove the panels.

Anatoly Popov also realized he would have to answer personally to Premier Stalin if he let a Soviet National Treasure such as the Amber Room fall into the German Army's hands. Not only would he be sent to a Gulag, but his whole family, his wife and son, then his cousins, in-laws, and anyone else related to him would soon follow. All because Stalin despised Hitler. Stalin would never let the Amber Room become Hitler's personal trophy.

They were running short on time and ideas. Nothing appeared to work. Desperation was setting in. Popov and his workers even tried to remove the walls behind the panels, leaving the stone attached to the Amber Panels to no avail.

As they stood around the room trying to think of another possible way to remove the panels, eight year old Andrei Popov, Anatoly Popov' son suddenly burst into the room, running up to his father, jumping up into his arms.

"Papa" he said cheerily. "I can run everywhere. Up and down the halls. No one is here."

Anatoly had a reason to smile for the first time in weeks as he hugged his son. Andrei's mother, Anatoly's wife, had already been evacuated weeks ago along with her mother and father. Anatoly's son begged to stay with his father until he relented.

Anatoly held his son as his team huddled in the Amber Room one last time.

"Papa," said Andrei, pointing to the Amber Room walls he had viewed many times before. "Did you find a way to remove the pretty panels?" he asked in his innocent voice. His father had been discussing nothing but the panels with him for over a week.

Anatoly smiled at his son. "No, not yet." The others surrounding them just shrugged.

Andrei pointed to the panels and said aloud, "Presto, disappear."

Anatoly deliberated his sons comment for a moment. It was so simple. However, it would never work. On the other hand, would it? Nevertheless, it was the only way forward. "That's it," he said excitedly to his team. "We make them disappear."

His meager workforce thought Anatoly was acting irrational from the combination of long hours and the stress of the German Army just outside of town. "Anatoly," said a young woman who specialized in Amber. "Maybe you should sit down and rest awhile."

"No, no," he said, "You don't understand. We can hide the panels in plain sight. We can attempt trickery. Since the Amber walls are flat we can try to hide them behind a thin layer of wallpaper."

They each looked at the walls then each other. It was almost too simple. Why hadn't they thought of it sooner? Anatoly quickly dispatched his workers to the basement maintenance area, hoping they would find the necessary materials. Anatoly stayed behind with his son.

****

IN A MATTER OF hours, they had finished applying the last roll of wallpaper covering the exquisite Amber Room panels. Paintings from other galleries were hastily moved in and placed about the room as if it were just another exhibit in the Gallery. They only required the ruse to work for several days or possibly a week. At least until the Soviet troops could beat back the invaders and they could reclaim their Palace once more. Anatoly stood back and admired the work. He patted young Andrei on his head. "You should be proud my son. You provided us with a brilliant idea. Some day you will look back at what you helped save."

Andrei smiled up at his father just as German artillery and tank shells started hurtling into the Palace exterior walls. A rather gruff army lieutenant from the 23rd Army suddenly poked his head into the room, his disheveled uniform attesting to the ongoing battle being fought around them. "We cannot hold the Palace," he said abruptly. "If we stay and try and defend it, the Germans will just destroy everything. In addition, I don't have enough troops to hold the bastards back. Therefore, I have ordered my remaining troops to evacuate back towards the city. I want all of you to head to the truck, now! Evacuate!"

Anatoly quickly thanked the lieutenant before he turned his attention to his workers who had gathered about him. "The Army has saved one military truck for our use to escape the German assault," he said as he looked from person to person, nodding his thanks for their assistance.

Shells were now tearing into the walls at a rate of one per second.

They had no choice. It was time to leave.

****

AT A STAGING ground only two kilometers from the Catherine Palace, newly minted Captain Stefan Weber, German Army Group North, nervously waited for the German artillery barrage to cease. A small man, shy, with a shock of premature greying hair. This was the closest he had dared approach the actual 'Front'.

Weber had arrived on the Russian Front only seven days ago when German forces stood ready to break the stalemate that had ensued since late August. Formerly Weber was one of Berlins top museum curators, in charge of the famed Schloss Charlottenburg. He was drafted for the sole purpose of pilfering the Catherine Palaces most prized artifact: the Amber Room.

Weber adjusted his field glasses to take in the majestic view of the Catherine Palace bathed in its blue and white splendor. *My God*, he thought to himself, *the palace was huge at almost ½ a kilometer in length!* Up until this point he had only read or seen pictures of the palaces splendor but viewing it in person he was truly amazed. Now he had to ensure the carefully planned window of opportunity didn't slam shut. Weber was uncertain if the conditions would be safe enough for his mission to be completed.

14

His unique assignment was provided to him directly from Albert Speer, Hitler's chief architect. Speer had informed Weber that it was Hitler's vision to install the prized Amber Room as the center piece of his new Fuhrermuseum to be built when the war ended. Now it was all up to Weber.

As with the other countries of Europe the Nazis had invaded, they systematically plundered its cultural property. It was so systemic that they even set up an organization known as the The Reichsleiter Rosenberg Institute for the Occupied Territories, or ERR, headed by Alfred Rosenberg. The ERR was specifically created to determine which public and private collections were most valuable to the Nazi Regime. Some of the objects were earmarked for Hitler's Fuhrermuseum, some objects went to other high-ranking officials such as Hermann Goering, while other objects were traded on the open market to fund Nazi activities.

Weber had no intention of being a hero. He was solely focused on finding the Amber Room intact, make haste its exit from the Soviet Union — and get everyone home safely.

To aid him in his mission, Weber had been assigned a team of museum curators and two amber experts; twenty in total, who, like himself, were inducted temporarily into the German Army for the duration of the Amber Room movement back to Prussia or possibly Germany. Well, all but one were temporarily inducted. One man, Dr. Alfred Rohde, world-renowned Amber expert and curator of Königsberg Castle, was added to his team at the last moment. It was rumored that he held Hitler's ear, even having visited Hitler's home in Berchtesgaden on one or two occasions. It was during one of these visits he made Hitler aware of the Amber Room and its significance. It was even rumored that Rohde promised Hitler the room for his Fuhrermuseum. And this was why he was placed as the sole *'civilian'* on the team.

Weber had his suspicions about the man but kept them mostly to himself. He had no choice. Upon successful completion of his mission he was promised a hasty return to his cushy job. He wouldn't jeopardize that. Moreover, he was not used to such austere living conditions. The night before he and his team slept in a former pig barn while Dr. Rohde slept in the comfort of a farmers house. This compliments of the commanding General.

****

WITHIN A MATTER of hours, the Palace was easily overrun. Most troops had wisely chosen to evacuate but there were still a few diehards who refused to retreat. Most notably, former Catharine Palace workers who were recently conscripted into the Army. They felt a certain allegiance to the Palace. Luckily for Captain Weber one of the few female soldiers who were captured was a former palace curator who was familiar with the location of the Amber Room.

A diminutive woman, all of five foot two, was harshly shoved in front of Weber by two German soldiers from another unit; a combat unit. He looked at her soot and grime covered uniform, blood from a gash on her forehead covered one side of her face. She stood defiantly, as if daring him to shoot her.

One of the soldiers spoke up. "This little Soviet witch shot dead three of our best men before she was knocked unconscious from a grenade blast."

Weber looked admiringly at the young woman, possibly 30, his own age. However, it was hard to really tell with her disheveled hair and the blood that covered the side of her face.

"Let her go," he ordered the soldiers.

The soldiers were ready to protest when Weber unbuttoned his holster for his sidearm. Wisely, they obeyed his order. "Let her be your responsibility, Sir," one soldier spat out in reply as they both turned and at a fast pace returned to their unit.

The woman soldier almost seemed relieved to be out of their care, knowing what cruelty such soldiers were capable of, having heard horror stories from her units Political Officer.

Weber pated down his pockets in search of hanky, a smile creased his face when he located one in his tunic's pocket. He opened it up to its full size before he applied some water from his canteen, in effect soaking it. He then motioned with the hanky to the cut on her forehead.

She had no choice as she simply nodded in response.

Weber dabbed at the blood, now dried, on her face and forehead. He kept smiling at her as to not alarm her. "I will not hurt you," he said, his units' translator translating his words for him. After several minutes, with the blood and grim mostly removed, her true Slavic beauty was revealed. Weber handed her the hanky. She slowly used it to clean the dirt from her hands, before handing it back to him.

A slight smile escaped her lips in thanks. She still stood staring defiantly at him.

Weber admired her courage as she stood before him and his rag-tag group of recently inducted *soldiers*. If the situation were reversed, he would have been begging for his life by now. "Allow me to introduce myself," he said, his eyes never leaving hers. "Captain Stefan Weber, museum curator in charge of the Schloss Charlottenburg in Berlin."

The prisoner had a look of shock spread across her face before his translator had even finished. She knew of this man. She had even met him once at the Schloss Charlottenburg when she was studying in Berlin before the war. He was well regarded in the small world of Museum Curators.

Weber then offered her a small piece of Handkase cheese and a portion of Landbrot, or farmers bread, from his mess kit. The prisoner grabbed both greedily when offered from his outstretched hands, having not eaten in days.

Weber waited until she was finished, then offered her his canteen. She took it gratefully. After several seconds she handed it back to him, again she allowed a slight smile to escape her lips.

She extended her hand. "Misha Petrov," she said confidently. "I was one of the Catherine Palaces many curators," she said in near perfect German. "That is before you and your Nazi bastards put me out of a job." She now defiantly eyed each of the soldiers who stood around her. She pointed up at the exterior of the Palace. "This is a historical monument for the world to see. It will take many years to repair the damage your many tank and artillery rounds have caused."

Weber nodded as he pointed to his little group. "We are not soldiers," he said. "We are curators, historians, and amber experts. We could never damage something so beautiful."

Misha looked at their uniforms. "You are Nazis," she spat out.

"No, we were civilians up until several weeks ago," replied one of Weber's men. "Much like yourself I would presume."

Misha had never even fired a weapon nevertheless seen one until a week ago when she was handed a uniform two sizes too big along with a rifle. "You're drafted," were the words she remembered from the burly sergeant.

"We are here to preserve one of your museums valuables," said Weber. If we don't the soldiers who follow us they will only destroy it. My orders are to save the Amber Room."

Misha's eyes went wide at the mention of the Amber Room. She had worked on the opposite side of the Museum in the Catherine jewelry collection but had viewed the Amber Room on numerous occasions. "Why would you want to save a Soviet treasure?" she asked.

"Because we are not soldiers," he said, "as I said earlier we are just like yourself, only in different uniforms." He pointed to the front steps. "There are over a thousand rooms in this place. It is going to take us a few hours to locate the Amber Room. Therefore, this is my offer. I promise if you lead us to the Amber Room, I will set you free."

Misha eyed him for a moment. She realized she had no choice. They could just kill her. Then, they would eventually find the room on their own.

"You are going to protect it?" She said in a low voice.

"You have my word," replied Weber, his hand outstretched.

Misha paused several seconds before she shook his hand. She then pointed to the steps. "If you follow me, it's about a fifteen minute walk from here."

Weber allowed Misha to lead the way up the marble State Staircase with its ornate banisters and reclining marble cupids. At the top of the steps, they entered the Great Hall, also referred to as the Hall of Light, which ran the entire length of the palace. At one time large arched windows, now blown out, provided light to see the gilded stucco that decorated the interior walls. They walked past room after room of elaborately furnished areas, then dining rooms, more sitting rooms, before finally reaching the room where the Amber Room had stood untouched for centuries.

Misha held up her hand and stopped them only meters from the room. She pointed down to where a hair thin trip wire stretched across the hallway. "I may have recently been drafted and a soldier for only week but I saw the Soviet Sappers installing these little bastards all over the palace."

Weber nodded his thanks. "We would have surely walked into that one," he said. He then turned to one of his men. "Return to the outside get an explosives expert. We need this diffused immediately."

Misha pointed to the next room. "This is it," she said proudly. "The Amber Room."

"Watch your step over the trip wire," said Weber, as his group stepped over the wire located only ½ meter off the parquet floor.

Upon entering the room, Weber and his men looked at each other and then the ornate wallpaper that decorated the walls. On the walls hung 18th century oil paintings spaced evenly about the room. Weber looked to Misha for an explanation.

"This is it," she said confidently. She looked around the room before walking into the hallway and then back into the room. "I swear this is where the Amber Room is, or was. On several occasions I worked just down the hall. You must believe me. I know this palace like the back of my hand."

Weber had a strict timetable. His orders were for him to have the Amber Room loaded and ready to go within 48 hours. This was the timeframe provided to him by the group commander. He was informed that the German troops in this sector could only keep the Soviets on the defensive for, at most, two days. After that, with no German reinforcements, the Soviets would conceivably force them back. Weber withdrew his Lugar from its holster and placed it against Misha's head. "Where is the Amber Room," he demanded, his earlier demeanor now gone. "You said you know where it was. You are of no use to me if you are lying. Don't make me shoot you."

Misha recognized something was odd. She had never seen this type of wallpaper used in the main building. It was typically used to decorate the guest rooms located in the rear of the palace courtyard. Never in the main museum rooms. "I swear, sir," she pleaded, "this is where the Amber Room was located. I visited the room only last month. They couldn't have moved it."

By now, all of Weber's little army were in the room, most admiring the paintings from well-known Russian artists that lined the walls. Weber repeated his words to Misha. "I am not a killer but this is your last chance. You are of no use to me if you are lying."

She shook her head. "This is the room," she stated once more. "It has to be."

Weber eyed Misha before turning to his men. "I want each of you to fan out and search the rooms on either side of this room and the ones across the hall. This palace is so large maybe we have the wrong room. And watch out for that damn trip wire!"

One of Webber's men noticed a nick in a section of the wallpaper, something glittering underneath. Curiosity caught the best of him as he walked over to the wall, rapping on it with his knuckles, feeling something may be hidden behind the paper. He pulled at the nick in the wallpaper only to have a small golden spot appear. "Captain," he said with urgency in his voice. "Something is underneath this paper."

Weber joined the man, eyeing the section of wallpaper that had been pulled up. He removed a pocketknife from his pants, scrapping a larger piece of paper off the wall. His eyes went wide. "All of this paper comes down, now," he ordered.

Within an hours' time Weber viewed the exquisite Amber panels that laid hidden beneath the wallpaper. He turned to Misha: "Please accept my apologies, Misha Petrov," bowing slightly. "You were correct. My men and I will take great care of your Amber Room panels." He then turned to his lead sergeant. "I want you to personally escort Miss Misha Petrov to safety. Provide her with a sidearm and enough food and water to last at least two days."

The sergeant snapped to attention." Yes, sir," he replied. "Follow me, miss."

Misha turned to Weber as she was about to be escorted from the room. "I don't wish you goodwill, but I do hope to someday visit the Schloss Charlottenburg in Berlin."

"When you do, you will be my personal guest," replied Weber to a departing Misha.

****

THE SOVIET RUSE hadn't fooled the German soldiers/curators, who, with the proper equipment, were able to remove the Amber Room panels within 36 hours, pack it up in wooden crates and ship it to Königsberg, Prussia where it was decided the room would be installed in the Konigsberg castle museum.

It was to be a temporary exhibition, only until the new Fuhrermuseum was built in Linz, Austria with *an expected opening in 1946.*

CHAPTER 2

August 31, 1945

Remnants of Königsberg Castle, Prussia.

The fortress of Königsberg was originally founded in the year of our Lord, 1255 by the Knights of the Teutonic Order in the course of their development of the Baltic region. They desired the location due to its prime location near the Pregel River, an important trading waypoint for European and Russian goods. At first the location merely consisted of earthen works, then as it became more populous, wood fortifications. With the discovery of vast amber deposits in the surrounding areas it was not long before stonemasons were employed elevating it to a true castle status. From 1457 onwards, it became the primary residence for Prussian Rulers. Over the course of the next 300 years, the castle was altered and enlarged numerous times to accommodate the growing aristocracy. The first major build was a west wing addition to contain the palace church where future Prussian Princes would be crowned.

Above the church they constructed one of the largest halls in all of Germany and Prussia, almost 235 feet in length by 50 feet across with a ceiling height of 55 feet. Then surrounding the inner castle walls, numerous apartments were added to house the Prussian rulers and their court. A hundred years later, a gothic tower that rose to a majestic 300 feet, towering over the city below it, was built within its walls. At the time it was considered the tallest structure in northeast Europe.

But by 1918, with the end of WWI and the German defeat, the Prussian monarchy had been ordered to dissolve. With its defeat, its majestic apartments were no longer needed to house the ruling Prussians, and the Castle was turned into a museum for over 250,000 exhibits of the Prussian era.

By 1937, the Nazis saw the value in a castle that provided awe-inspiring settings, holding torchlight rallies in its courtyards and beer parties in its massive hall for its followers. Fast forward to 1941 and Germany entering a war with the Soviet Union: the castle now became Himmler's eastern Headquarters when Hitler was in his Wolfs Lair compound, 8 km east of the small East Prussian town of Rastenburg. Himmler wanted nothing to do with the mosquito infested site, preferring his comforts in the Königsberg Castle.

Four years later, this is where Dr. Alfred Rohde, world-renowned Amber expert and curator of Königsberg Castle now stood, or what remained of the castle after the previous nights Allied bombing raid. As smoke rose around him from the various castle buildings charred timbers, their many roofs collapsed, their gables crumbling, his bony white hand held the latest directive from Adolf Hitler that declared that all looted possessions from the city of Königsberg were to be sent directly to Germany for safekeeping. Hitler wanted to keep anything of value from the advancing Soviets hands, notably Stalin.

Rohde absently tugged on his Fedora. *You are a little late*, he thought as he looked around in despair for the works of art he could not rescue. Or the many civilians who had sought shelter within the castles walls.

He crumpled the Hitler Directive and tossed it to the ground in utter disgust. He knew it was only a matter of days before the Russians would completely encircle the city. But Rohde was a very wise, or some would say foolish man. He had chosen not to wait for a Hitler Directive. He used his own initiative and had moved the Castles *'eighth wonder of the world'* three months ago. Something that could have gotten him shot if discovered.

Originally when the Germans captured or stole the Amber Room from Leningrad's Catherine Palace, it was reassembled and put on display in the Königsberg castle museum. That was in 1941, when the German Army was sweeping across Europe and the Soviet Union. Then, in 1944, the tide had changed drastically. The Allies were moving closer to victory each day. Rohde realized the obvious and that the castle would eventually become a prime target for Allied bombers. Fortunately for the art-loving world, in May of 1944, Rohde had instructed his workers to close the Amber Room gallery for maintenance. At least that was his ruse. He was not waiting for the authorities to inform him how to protect one of the world's most valuable treasures.

But he required a place to store them outside of the Castle. Someplace no one would suspect.

By coincidence one Sunday in May 1944, after attending mass at St. Joseph's Church, a Roman Catholic Church in the Ponarth quarter of Königsberg, he had overheard his fellow worshipers speak of the churches basement and how it could be used in time of emergency as an air raid shelter. He heard them say its walls were over one meter thick and contained a storage area over 50 meters in length by 50 meters in width. In addition, with the church located just on the edge of the city's historic district, it would hopefully be out of harm's way.

Rohde soon requested the St. Joseph's church pastor, Father Fritz Gause, to tour the church's basement. Father Gause nodded to the simple request. He even included another priest; a small almost gnomish man who at the time was busy extinguishing the churches alter candles. "Do you mind if he also accompanies us?" Father Gause had asked.

Rohde laughed aloud. "Father it is your church. Invite the whole parish if need be."

The priest he pointed to was Antonio Perluci of the Vatican Intelligence staff, secretly visiting on the sole hopes of a meeting with Dr. Alfred Rohde. Now the man had come to him. *It was divine providence.*

Father Gause led the way down the narrow stone steps, Rohde behind him, closely followed by Perluci. At the bottom of the steps, Father Gause flicked on the basement lights, one by one, until the whole room lay bathed in artificial light.

Rohde immediately realized the potential of the large concrete space. "I need this room," he said aloud to no one in particular, "I want this room."

Father Gause pointed over to a back room, its door padlocked. "There is a smaller room behind the door that can also be made available for you," he said.

"No, this will do nicely," he said in reply. "I only have 25 wooden crates of a medium size." He used his hands to convey the approximate size of the crates.

Perluci smiled as he first turned to Father Gause, then to Dr. Rohde. "Perhaps we can do business," he said, secretly thanking God for *bringing the rat to the cheese.*

Within days the Amber Room panels were moved in a three-truck convoy to St. Josephs, *for safekeeping and maintenance.*

****

ROHDE WAS PRUDENT in his thinking. Over the course of the next six months, the towns' historic district, including the part of Königsberg castle that had originally stored the Amber room, were destroyed in a series of British and Russian bomber raids.

St. Joseph's Church was miraculously spared.

Dr. Alfred Rohde had chosen his location well. *Or so he had thought.*

CHAPTER 3

Present Day - Florida Keys, United States

Many a worldly traveler referred to the Florida Keys as *the American Caribbean Isles* because the Keys happen to feature many of the same amenities as its tropical brethren: deep blue skies, warm turquoise ocean waters, crystal white beaches, swaying palm trees, and the ever present boozed up tourists. But the one thing the Keys possessed that its uptight, Caribbean island neighbors did not: *it had a laid-back feel*. Almost like a 1960s vibe reverberating through the Island chain. San Francisco if it were warm and had access to fabulously sunny beaches.

The Craggy Dog Marina was a suitable fit with its Keys neighbors, as it contained all the fundamentals the new generation of baby-boomer retirees necessitated for their vacation abodes: a freshwater lap pool with a swim-up bar, tennis courts, private beach, and a 200-foot pier suitable for fishing. At every turn you could view palm trees softly swaying with the continuous warm ocean breeze, each tall and wide enough to provide shade where desired. To top it off, the weather hovered around a constant 85 to 90 degrees.

Now, only 12 boats lay moored to the Craggy Dogs piers, a number that could easily reach a peak of 30 when the *snowbirds* from Pennsylvania, New York, and New Jersey returned in winter. The boats currently tied up ranged from a "low-end" 23-foot King Fisher sail boat to a "high-end" 57-foot Jefferson Motor Yacht with the name "Irish Rebel" painted conspicuously in emerald green on its stern.

The Irish Rebel lay moored at the end of the dock just past a near empty beach, and the beach lounge that sat just beyond it. The stools at the bar were rumored to have the best view of the sun as it dipped below the horizon.

****

A TALL MAN walked down the wooden dock towards the Irish Rebel, he struggled to balance a case of Corona Light and a bag of limes he had unwisely placed on top of the case of beer. The well-built man was dressed in what was accepted as the local dress code: leather sandals, baggy white shorts, a Hawaiian print shirt, and on top of his buzz cut, a beat up Panama hat. Eian Doherty, all of six feet and pushing a solid 220 pounds had an ear-to-ear grin as he approached the Irish Rebel. His once handsome face attested to the fact that at one time he liked to box. But with injuries and age he was forced to give up the sport and apply his energies into something he could really enjoy: gambling. He loved it. That and flying. But in gambling circles he was known as an easy mark; a whale. Luckily his job as a corporate pilot kept him, for the most part, out of the *hole* for his gambling losses. Only two days ago Eian was in Philadelphia to square off his latest debt with the Philly Irish Mob when he had received Jim Dieters call.

With his debts paid off he was free and clear of everyone, for the moment; *well, with the exception of the FBI, Interpol, or the British SAS.*

Eian ambled up the short gangway to the Irish Rebel, careful not to lose his plastic bag full of fresh limes. As he stepped onto the yacht, he paused for a moment to look fore and aft. He knew life was good. At only 35 years of age, he had come a long way from living in an Irish tenement house in Belfast during *the troubles.*

The "Irish Rebel" could easily sleep eight, with a full galley, three bathrooms or *heads* in nautical speak, teak decking throughout, and a small two-person hot tub on the stern. Rumors circulated about the origins of its previous owner's wealth, with him now dead. Nevertheless, it didn't stop the rumors. The truth has nothing on a good rumor. The best one circulating amongst the Craggy Dog crowd was the previous owner stole some Nazi gold. However, no one knew for sure.

Eian walked into the main salon, eying the new boats owner and his business partner, Jim Dieter, as he sat at the dining salons table with his wife of a only a few months, Nora Robinson. They were in a deep discussion before they noticed his entrance.

Jim and Nora jumped up from their seats to greet the newcomer.

Eian handed the case of beer to Jim. "Never come empty handed my old mum use to say." He handed the bag of limes to Nora. Each took their turn in hugging Eian in greeting. "Glad you could make it," said Dan as he pointed to the table, an empty wine glass marked his spot.

Jim placed the case of beer by the Galley door; he took the limes from Nora and placed them on top of the case. "This will be for later," he said. "We can enjoy them on the top deck after we get this little situation out of the way."

Eian's ears perked up. "When you tell me there is a situation, Jimmy, I get worried," he said, a smile creasing his face. "But usually it's *a lucrative situation.*"

Jim Dieter sat back down at the small, round dining table, stretching out his legs. At 6'2', 210 pounds, he carried himself with easy self-assurance. His brown hair, tinged with grey, was thick with willfulness that expensive cutting had not completely disciplined. This combined with his rugged features and a physique he maintained from his Naval Academy days drew many a passing stare. He picked up the newly opened bottle of Merlot and walked around the table to where his wife sat with a smile gracing her face. "Thank-you, sir," she said playfully, as he poured some Merlot into her empty glass. Nora stood 5 '8, with long shoulder length hair that seemed to constantly battle between blonde with brown roots and brown; a lithe body, and what captured men most of all were her eyes: a deep pool of blue-green. They seemed even greener as Jim looked down appreciatively at her.

Jim held up an expensive bottle of Merlot, and then he pointed to an empty glass on the table. Eian took note.

"Don't want to be a damp rag on the party," he said before choosing to sit down.

Jim quickly filled up his glass and placed the bottle down in front of him. Wasting no time, he then picked up his glass in toast. "To our dear departed friend, Dan Flaherty, may he rest in peace." He clinked glasses with Nora and Eian. When they were done, Jim held up a thin manila envelope for Eian to see. Jim chose not to open it until Eian had arrived from Philly. Jim eyed the envelope for several minutes before he spoke in a low voice. "This was addressed to me. Dan left it in a conspicuous spot on the boat knowing that if he died I would easily find it."

"Yeah, he left it on the bar," said Nora sarcastically. "You don't have be so overly dramatic. Open it."

Dan smiled at his wife's take on events. "I promised my darling wife that I would wait for you to arrive before I opened it."

"Well I'm here. Don't keep us in suspense, Jim, open it."

Nora nodded. "It's time, Jim," she said. "We are all curious what Dan's last words were."

Jim felt melancholy. He realized once he opened it, Dan was truly dead. This would be his last communication with his friend. Jim tried his best to muster a smile as he ripped open the envelopes top. He peaked inside before he turned the envelope upside down, dumping its contents on the table in front of them. Out fell two smaller envelopes, one addressed to him, the other to a woman named Shannon Flaherty, Castletownbere, Ireland.

Not familiar with the name, he set the envelope aside for later, opening the one addressed to him. Inside he found a two page handwritten letter dated nine weeks ago. "He wrote this just before we left for Lebanon," said Jim. He started to read the letter aloud so Nora and Eian could hear it as well. In it, Dan admitted killing the former Vatican point man Perluci, and how he dumped his body overboard. He said he had to do it. Dan said the man was unscrupulous and would have eventually turned on them. Nevertheless, before he killed him he was able to extract a detailed confession from Perluci not only about the Bormann treasure they had located in Lebanon, but also about another treasure Perluci was going to keep for himself but had second thoughts. Dan went on to say once Perluci knew he was going to die he couldn't stop the man from chatting. Perluci went on and on about all of his exploits from around the world. How he screwed the Soviets, the Nazis, even his employers, The Vatican. How he, and he alone was able to steal the eighth wonder of the world from under their very noses, and keep it for himself! In addition, he said Perluci even told him the exact location.

That was the end of the letter. Jim looked on the back of the letter, in the envelope, to no avail. "I can't believe this," he said aloud holding the last page of the letter. "Dan knew the location of whatever the eighth wonder of the world was but didn't tell me. Is this some joke from the grave?" He wouldn't put it past him. Dan was the biggest practical jokester of them all. He promptly thought of the time Dan released 20 Geckos in Eian's room while he was sleeping. Eian hated snakes and lizards. When he woke, he screamed so loud you would have thought he was on fire.

Dan placed the letter back in its envelope before he grabbed his smart phone and googled 'Eighth wonder of the world'. In a matter of seconds, he had his answer.

"You're not going to believe this," he said aloud. "I think he found the location of the Amber Room!"

CHAPTER 4

June 1944: St. Joseph's Church, Königsberg

Father Gause and Antonio Perluci stood in the relative safety of the church's basement, admiring the wooden crates that lay stacked in neat rows before them, the Amber Room contents packed carefully inside.

Father Gause was the first to speak, his eyes not moving from the wooden crates. "Is this what you were sent here to accomplish?" he asked, already knowing the response. "The Holy Father sent you here just for this?"

Perluci simply nodded, a smile creasing his face.

Father Gause turned in time to view Perluci's expression of delight. He despised the Vatican's employ of people such as Perluci but realized in some cases, such as this one, it was a necessity. "I have no desire to know the details," he said. "Do what you have to but don't apprise me of any of the details. I want to be able to honestly inform Dr. Rohde that I knew nothing of the theft."

Perluci nodded once more. "He won't know a thing," he said. Perluci's job was simple: he was on a mission for the Vatican to lay the groundwork to see if a deal could be undertaken with Dr. Rohde for the Amber Room. His employers had authorized him to offer up to $2 million in Vatican gold bars on deposit at the Vatican Bank. Possibly even safe passage for him and his wife to escape not only the Nazis but the rapidly approaching Soviet Army. If he chose to accept, the Vatican would secretly move its newly acquired treasure to the relative safety of Vatican City. If not, Rohde was to be blackmailed.

Perluci had used his time wisely since he first arrived in Königsberg several weeks ago. He covertly shadowed Rohde on his many travels around town in order to ascertain his likes or dislikes. Women, booze, high living. It didn't matter. Perluci was soon frustrated that Rohde had none of these propensities. The man simply went to work, went home to his wife, and attended church on Sundays. Blackmail wouldn't work on someone such as Rohde.

However, just when he was about to give up, divine intervention reared its ugly head. Rohde approached them requiring a safe place to hide the Amber Room. Perluci wouldn't even have to make a deal. It was presented to him giftwrapped. Rohde didn't even ask for security. He merely requested that the basement door be locked at all times and he would visit once a month. He had no desire to draw any unnecessary attention to the treasure.

Of course, Perluci and Gause readily agreed to Rohde's simple demands.

To think the eighth wonder of the world and one of the world's most lucrative treasures was sheltered in a church basement with a simple key-operated lock as security.

Now Perluci only had to steal the Amber Room from under the very nose of Rohde, hide the fact he had done so, and drive the treasure through a thousand kilometers of Nazi occupied territory.

If only life could be so simple.

CHAPTER 5

Present day: Beirut, Lebanon

Beirut would seem to have it all: a cosmopolitan society, beach resorts, mountains, friendly weather, good food and wine, and vibrant bars.

Known as the party capital of the Arab world, Beirut is a freewheeling city where Gulf Arabs, expatriates, and Lebanese émigrés fly in to enjoy its luxury hotels. However, under the veneer of modernism lie sectarian demons coiled to strike.

With the assassination of Sheik Hassan Nasrallah only weeks ago, the one-time leader of Lebanon's Shiite movement Hezbollah — an attack almost universally blamed on Israel and the American James Dieter — brought the merry-go-round to a juddering halt.

Gunmen and protesters filled the streets, reflecting the antagonisms fueling the conflict in next-door Syria and

THE VATICAN'S FINAL SECRET by FRANCIS JOSEPH SMITH

reviving memories of the sectarian hatreds that sunk Lebanon into its 1975 to 1990 civil war, a conflict whose wounds have far from healed.

Sheik Hassan Nasrallah's followers were in the process of providing a "Martyr's" funeral for its controversial leader; a funeral that should have been held soon after his death but his DNA was only recently identified.

Militants with AK-47s strapped across their chest helped to man checkpoints as Nasrallah's coffin, draped in the movement's yellow-and-green flag, was carried to its burial place in the capitals Ghobeiri area, a bastion of Hezbollah support. A thick crowd chanted "Death to Israel! Death to America!" and waved the Palestinian, Lebanese and Hezbollah flags, as the coffin was carried to a mausoleum reserved for "Martyrs".

The new Hezbollah leader, Sheik Naim Quasson, marched alongside Nasrallah's coffin. For many years Nasrallah's group held the distinction for killing more Americans than any other terrorist group until September 2001, when Al Qaeda assumed that role. Long considered one of the CIAs toughest adversaries, Hezbollah had for years been improving their ability to hunt and kill its enemies.

Sheik Naim Quasson knew his group had to seek revenge for Sheik Hassan Nasrallah's murder. First on their list was to execute the American James Dieter whom they now considered an agent of Israel.

****

THE FUNERAL LONG over, Sheik Naim Quasson returned to his opulent home located in the western section of the city. Said to have been originally designed by a long dead Italian architect, the house was sheltered from the bustling street by a high stone wall and citrus trees. Inside one is greeted by traditional Lebanese arches, trompe l'oeil marble walls, real marble floors, and a bright turquoise ceiling some 20 feet high.

The Sheik nodded in greeting to his butler, the butler pointing over a young man admiring a series of painted wall panels replicating illustrations of fables from a 15th-century Persian manuscript that lined the hallway. "He has arrived, sir," he said crisply. The Sheik walked over to his guest, the young man intrigued by the artwork, not noticing as he stood beside him.

The Sheik spoke in a low voice: "All of this was created by the Belgian artist, Isabelle de Borchgrave. I commissioned her several years ago to create something very unique, yet very religious."

The young man nodded in admiration. "You have succeeded. I must consider her for something in my own home."

"I will provide you with her contact information after we have concluded our business. He motioned for the man to follow him to the rear of his house, walking past a 19th-century painted-wood bookcase in the room that looked as though it served as the Sheik's den, following him to the rear of his house and onto his stone patio. His two young children played in the in-ground salt-water pool. The Sheik waved to them before turning to face his guest,

"Please sit," he said. Once they were seated, the butler once again returned.

"Bring us some fruit juice, please," ordered the Sheik, waiting until the butler left to continue.

"I have a job for you," he said to the young man. The young man being Hassan Talif, a 20-something who had performed numerous assassinations for the Sheik over a two-year period. His light skin, almond eyes, and good looks allowed him to blend in most Western countries, making him the ideal hit man.

"I want you to go to Ireland and work with some of our friends in the Irish Republican Army or what is commonly referred to as the IRA," said the Sheik.

Hassan looked at the Sheik, a puzzled look upon his face. "I thought the IRA went the way of the rotary phone? Didn't they disestablish over a decade ago?"

The Sheik held up his hands in response. "To answer your question, it's a bit of a yes and no. Supposedly they went away to satisfy the Good Friday peace agreement. However, our particular friends in the IRA would have nothing to do with the agreement and decided to go underground and, with our funding, still perform our business. The people I am sending you to are to be trusted and have performed shall we say, *some high-end missions*, both in Ireland and on the continent. As with most westerners, they work more for the money," he paused, as he smiled at Hassan, "unlike true believers, who work more for the cause. I have had my subordinates prepare the groundwork for your journey. Our contacts have also been notified to expect you."

At that moment, as if on cue, a tall, well-built man in a cream-colored suit walked onto the patio, looking first to the Sheik, the Sheik nodded to him, the man then handed Hassan a white folder. As the man leaned down Hassan noticed the shoulder strap holding in-place a small foldable stock machine gun. He was obviously the Sheik's aide and personal bodyguard. Hassan knew that the Sheik was on the top of the Israelis' hit list so he had to be careful.

The Sheik pointed to the folder. "In there you will find an airline ticket, a list of our IRA contacts, and twenty thousand euros for expenses." He paused for a moment, before he motioned to his aide. "Leave us." Once the aide had departed, a sly grin crept across the Sheiks face before speaking: "We all can't work for free in these hostile times. It is understood that we must all have a little safety net to carry us through the turbulent times. So in that spirit, a deposit has been made into your Geneva account for the usual amount."

Hassan nodded purposefully, knowing the Sheik to be a man of his word. "I will do as you say. And I will also memorize the list of IRA contacts before burning them. No need putting our allies in danger. We both know the Israelis' have their agents located everywhere. I even have some in my own group. Which, over time, I will methodically find and eliminate them. As for the job you have so graciously assigned me, hopefully within the week, with Gods will, it will be done."

"You understand that this job *must* be done within the week? I do not want to hear this *hopefully* within the week message you are telling me."

Hassan was taken back by the Sheiks change of tone. "Yes, sir," he replied meekly. "I will do as you say."

The Sheik could see he had upset his guest. He smiled at him and in a conciliatory voice said: "My rationale is this my young friend. From what my sources tell me the word is out on the street about Dieter and the Israelis. Our enemies might help this man escape our type of justice. We cannot let this happen. Even more disturbing is the fact that I also hear the Vatican is thinking about getting involved. The Vatican! Can you believe such nonsense? They also want Dieter dead. So that makes for a crowded field. I want us to be responsible for the killing of this man just to save our reputation. What happens to those who get in our way is Allah's will."

"I understand completely, sir."

The Sheik eyed Hassan for a moment before continuing. "Do whatever it takes. And I mean, *whatever it takes*, to get this job done. I want revenge for our brother warrior. I want revenge for his family. I want revenge for Allah."

"Allah Akbar," Hassan said before holding up the folder, patting it once. "His will be done, brother," he said before he stood up, shook hands with the Sheik and departed.

Once he had left, the Sheik wasted no time in picking up his cell phone, calling one of his numerous contacts. The cell phone rang twice before someone answered on the opposite end. "The little bird is in flight. You will provide him with whatever services he requires," he said, "Do you understand?"

45

"Absolutely, sir," replied the voice in a harsh Belfast accent. "As agreed beforehand, you deposit the funds into our account and you can have whatever you want."

The Sheik smiled at the greediness of the man. "It is already done," he said before he hung up.

He knew his 'little bird' would succeed.

CHAPTER 6

Present Day - Florida Keys, United States

Eian had a smile from ear to ear. "If cousin Dan really was able to gain the location of the Amber Room from Perluci before he killed him, we could be in for a nice payday."

Jim held up Dan's letter. "We still have one little problem," he said. "Doesn't mean a thing unless we find out where Dan hid the information. It could be somewhere on this boat, in a bank lock box. Who knows?"

Nora nodded in agreement. "I would imagine it would be here on his boat," she said. "Maybe we should break up and search the boat?"

Eian reached for the envelope addressed to a woman named Shannon Flaherty in the town of Castletownbere, Ireland. "Or how about this person?"

"It's a definite possibility," said Nora.

"Are you thinking what I'm thinking?" Jim said to both Nora and Eian.

Nora thought about it for a moment. "Could be his sister." She turned to Eian, a man who boasted of Dan being his blood relative since they first met. "You would know more than us. Did he have a sister?"

Eian shook his head with a puzzled look about his face. "You know how Dan used to call me cousin, and we were, but third cousins at best. We were from different sections of Ireland. I didn't see much of him as kids growing up. We only became close when we joined *the cause*." Eian paused for a moment as if in deep thought. "I'm trying to remember if any of my Aunts and Uncles had ever mentioned a sister of Dan's." After a few seconds, he shook his head in surrender. "I'm sorry but I really don't recall. You know how secretive the bastard was. Even pertaining to his own family."

The inquisitive reporters' nature in Nora wouldn't give up. "Let's take a step back and go with a longshot. What if Dan had a daughter?"

Jim sat there dumbfounded. "Dan Flaherty with a daughter? You've got to be kidding? He never mentioned nor hinted of a family."

"Work with me here, Jim. It's the only rationale I can come up with," she replied. "She might be able to lead us to this Amber Room. She might even possess a clue and not be aware of its significance. She might even be the clue."

Jim held up the letter Dan had addressed to Shannon Flaherty. "No, you are right. If our friend Dan thought it was important enough to write a letter to this woman, we have to follow through and deliver it."

Eian nodded in agreement. "I agree with Nora," he said. "I bet she's the clue."

****

AT A BOAT DOCK two slips away, a powerfully built man sat inside the cabin of a 37-foot Monterey Sport boat. The inside of the boat was unkempt, with numerous empty Chinese food take-out boxes scattered about the cabin. The boat had pulled in two days ago and its owner hadn't even bothered to make an appearance on deck, at least during daylight hours. Even the shades were pulled down. Right now from the comfort of the boats cabin, he pointed a powerful, sonic, handheld listening device at the *Irish Rebel*. Used by most of the well-known agencies, its high sensitivity microphone had the capability to tune into sounds from over 500 feet away. With the *Irish Rebel* only 125 feet away, the conversations came in as if he were sitting in the room with his targets. Moreover, he had recorded them all. With mention of a possible daughter, the man sat up.

Now it was getting interesting.

****

"I HAVE AN IDEA," said Jim. He reached over and snatched Nora's phone from the table in front of her and dialed a number from memory. After two rings, a man picked up. "Ortiz, it's your favorite ex-teammate, Jim Dieter." After several minutes of good-natured give and take, Jim said: "I need a quick favor. You still work for Interpol?" After confirmation, he continued. "I need you to run the name Daniel Flaherty through your data base. He should be on the old IRA watch lists from the 70s and 80s. I need you to check to see if any known family pops up and their locations. I'm talking to you from a borrowed cell so you can reach me at the number you see on the caller ID."

Jim turned to Nora, handing back her phone. "That was a guy I knew from the SEALs. He went to work for the good guys, not the contractors. Let's give him a few minutes to work his magic and see what pops up."

"And you just happen to know his number from memory?" Nora said skeptically.

"Okay, I use him from time to time," he said.

Nora continued to stare at him, not speaking.

"I said from time to time. He's a friend. Don't you talk to your friends? It's not like it's another woman. I make it a point to talk to him every couple of months. He has a lot of good insight."

"You know I don't like secrets, she said. "Anything else you're keeping from me?"

Jim held up his hands. "No more secrets, promise."

After a couple of awkward minutes, Nora's cell phone rang. She looked at the caller ID. She handed it back to Jim. "Evidently it's for you," she said sarcastically.

Jim winked at Nora as he grabbed her phone. "What do you have for me, my friend?" On the other end, his friend spoke as Jim took notes. After several minutes he was done. "Thanks. I owe you a night on the town when you come to the states. Talk to you soon."

Jim handed Nora back her phone as a look of shock spread across his face. "You are not going to believe this," he said. "Dan does have a daughter and her name is Shannon Flaherty. She is 26 years old. Her mother is dead. Mother went by the name Maureen O'Dywer. She died last year after a short bout with cancer. Miss O'Dywer was evidently someone Dan had met when he was in the IRA. They were partners at one time. The British cleared her of any wrongdoing, pinning all crimes on Dan."

"I don't want to sound like a prude," said Nora, "but if they had a daughter together I would say they were a bit more than partners."

Jim smiled at her suggestion before continuing. "And you are not going to believe this. She lives right outside Castletownbere on a plot of land called Sheep Hollows Farm. She evidently inherited the farm from her mom when she died."

Nora had a puzzled look on her face. "You said her name is Shannon Flaherty? Not O'Dywer like the mothers name?"

Jim looked at the notes he had taken. "Holy shit," he said, the name slowly sinking in. "She took Dan's last name and not her mother's. That could only mean she knew about Dan being her father. Either the mother told her or Dan and the mother lived together for a while."

"We have to pay this young lady a visit," said Nora.

Jim nodded in agreement. "I think we are leaving as soon as Eian can rent us a nice little eight seater. Is your commercial pilot's license out of hock yet?"

Eian turned to Jim and Nora. "I just got here. I didn't even get a swim in yet."

Jim laughed aloud. "Nora, we can't be impolite to our guest. You're right, Eian. How about we leave in two days' time. And then you can still fly us over the pond to your native soil."

Eian looked at him like he had two heads. "After my last rental that you destroyed, I'll be lucky if they rent us a Piper Cub." Of course he was referring to the 737 that Eian flew across the Atlantic landing at Millville, New Jersey that was destroyed in a firefight with British Commandos two months ago. Luckily for Eian it was deemed an accident by the FAA under strict orders at the highest authority.

"Stop your whining and rent us a small jet with departure out of Key West in two days. Offer up to double the usual rate if there is any blowup over the Millville incident. We still have a lot of money left over from the Bormann job."

****

TWO SLIPS AWAY the man inside the cabin of the 37-foot Monterey Sports boat couldn't believe his luck. He overheard the whole conversation. Since Jim, Nora, and Eian weren't leaving for another two days, it was still possible for his people to get a jump on them. He hit the redial button on his cell phone and reached his boss in a matter of seconds.

"Hassan, I have the information you require."

CHAPTER 7

Present day - Belfast, Ireland

Hassan Talif looked a bit out of his environment as he walked into O'Dwyers Pub. He stopped for a moment just inside the Pubs front door, his eyes adjusting to the interiors lighting. After a minute or so, he was able to admire the Pubs Victorian style with a heavy accent on dark woods. The pub was crowded for a Tuesday night; all of the stools at the bar were taken. Off to his left he noticed three comfortable looking leather chairs placed conveniently in front of an unlit fireplace, two of them presently occupied by his contacts: Kagen Sims, and Berk Logan.

Hassan had been warned by the Sheik before he left Lebanon that Sims and Logan were "old-school IRA", the kind who would kill merely for the money just to keep their organization going. Between the two of them, they had been credited for 16 killings, all since the end of the so-called hostilities. He also was aware that they had committed four bank robberies, two bombings and numerous acts of passing high-grade counterfeit bills, both euro and pound notes. Of course, all acts were committed in the name of the Irish Republican Army.

Sims tapped a napping Logan on the arm with a rolled up Belfast Telegraph newspaper. "I think our benefactor has arrived," he said in a heavy Irish brogue. Sims was first to rise from his chair, hastily followed by Logan, his hand extended in greeting, taking Hassan's in his own and pumping it enthusiastically.

"A pleasure to meet you, Mr. Talif," said Sims earnestly, knowing Hassan's benefactor was paying them handsomely.

"Please call me, Hassan," he said, a smile gracing his face from ear-to-ear. "The Sheik has told me many great things about you both. He mentioned to me you have done many great things for the cause in both Ireland and the United Kingdom."

"Hassan, you are too kind,' replied Logan. He pointed to the comfy seats by the fireplace. "Please, take a seat and let's discuss the details of our little venture."

Once they all were settled, Logan grabbed his beer, holding it up so the barmaid could see they all wanted another round. "Before we begin our business transaction, allow me to tell you a short story as to how Sims and myself ended up here," he said, his eyes never leaving Hassan's. "I just want to dispel any fears or misunderstandings you may have about the two of us."

Hassan nodded to his simple request.

Logan continued. "In 1969 Britain deployed its army to Northern Ireland for what was meant to be a brief peacekeeping operation. Well their definition is obviously different from mine. They stayed for 38 damn years, this as the Irish Republican Army mounted a guerrilla war against the state."

Logan paused as the server deposited three Guinness on the small glass table in front of them. "Thank-you, Katy my darling," he said, making it obvious he was a regular. He waited until she returned to her post by the bar before he continued in a much lower tone, never knowing who was listening, leaning in to Hassan. "Belfast was a war zone back in the day. Tanks rolled through the streets. Checkpoints sealed the major roads. Bombs and snipers' bullets felled civilians as they went about their ordinary activities. The attacks were brutal and swift."

Logan looked around the room as if a bit paranoid, also his demeanor seemed to change the more he spoke. He suddenly picked up his glass and raised it to Hassan and Sims, waiting for them to do the same. "Slancha," he said, taking a small sip before continuing. "The Good Friday Agreement of 1998 marked the official end of the *Troubles* as we like to call our little dispute with the British Empire. It required the decommissioning of all paramilitary groups, power sharing between unionists and nationalists in government, and — the part that caused the most controversy — the release of all people imprisoned for their role in the conflict. It meant that everyone walked free, from our low-level operatives in prison for a weapons charge to cold-blooded assassins such as Sims and myself who were sentenced to rot in jail only two years earlier.

And you may ask why we were in jail." He looked over to Sims, providing him with a chest high salute with his right hand. "Twenty three years ago, when we were just young lads of eighteen, we ambushed four soldiers along a quiet country road. Made a lot of press over here. Unfortunately we got caught."

Logan eyed Hassan for several more seconds as if to make a statement. "That's who we are, Hassan," he said, as he leaned back in his chair. "Do not confuse us with the rank and file amateurs you may have dealt with in the past. Between the two of us we have a lot of experience performing just the type of work you will require on our soil."

Hassan smiled as he raised his beer to toast them. "In Lebanon we say, *Kesak*," he said, their glasses clinking in toast before he took a sip. "Trust me when I say, I know exactly who you are." Hassan lifted his briefcase from the floor beside him and placed it on his lap. He then pointed down to the briefcase. "Do you have any idea what's in this case?" he asked.

Logan smiled at Sims, then Hassan. "I'm sure you will soon show us, Hassan," replied Logan. "Or", as he pointed up to the bar where two unsavory types sat eyeing Hassan, "our two friends will place a bullet in your head and simply take the case."

Hassan was prepared for this. It was his turn to smile. "Not a problem. I completely understand. You think I am just an olive skinned man who is a bit out of his element. But if you gentlemen will notice the man in the corner you will see I am not to be underestimated."

Logan and Sims turn to see a rather rough looking gentleman drinking a pint with one hand, in the other he had a newspaper placed over an Uzi machine gun, the gun pointed at the two men at the bar.

"Touché, gentlemen," says Hassan.

Logan and Sims burst out laughing as they slapped the table in front of them. "I like this man," said Logan.

"Good, I assume we are all friends again, yes," replied Hassan. He opened the briefcase and turned it towards Logan and Sims, ensuring only they had a clear view of its contents.

Both their eyes went wide. "That's a lot of cash, my friend," exclaimed Sims, "I think a bit more than we agreed upon."

Hassan nodded. "Yes, a little extra from what we previously agreed upon, in addition to what my boss already deposited into your account. But just the same it's all yours if you help me kidnap, James Dieter, and whoever is with him." He paused for a few seconds, looking at both Sims and Logan as they took the case and closed it quickly to keep from prying eyes. "Or, if need be, *to kill them.*"

"We would kill the Queen for the kind of cash you are paying," replied Sims, laughing as he said it but with a hint of seriousness in his voice.

Hassan beamed. "Well for the moment let's just stick with James Dieter and company."

Logan removed a sheet of folded-up paper from his pants pocket and handed it to Hassan. "I took the liberty of starting the research on our targets," he said with a mischievous grin. "Dieter and his little band of misfits are in the southwest of Ireland as we speak. My sources inform me he is attending to some unfinished business. We think it has to do with visiting one of his friends who died in a gunfight somewhere over in your territory."

Hassan beamed once more. "I have been told you two are the best. Now I am sure of it." Hassan eyed the neatly typed information on the paper. He then looked up at Logan and Sims as he nodded. The paper contained everything from the Private Aircraft Tail number Jim, Nora, and Eian had arrived on at Cork's Airport, the hotels they had stayed in, down to the meals they had eaten. "Very thorough, my new friends, very thorough indeed." He handed the paper back to Logan.

Logan pointed to the two rough looking men at the bar, each looking as though they played Irish Rugby for a living. "We have those two plus an additional three men already vetted that could help us at a moment's notice, if need be." He reached into his coats pocket, pulling out another sheet of paper, unfolding it before he handed it to Hassan. "Here is a list of the equipment we presently have available for your use. You will notice we have the standard M-16s, M-4s, AK-47s, and Uzi's; below that we have Rocket Propelled Grenades, fragmentation grenades, smoke grenades, anti-tank missiles; and of course the ones at the bottom, Stinger Anti-Aircraft Missiles, and an assortment of Armored vehicles. The bottom line equipment would require 24 hours to round them up and be delivered to your specified location."

Hassan smiled once more, impressed with his new partners. "Gentlemen, before I left Lebanon, I was briefed on your backgrounds. You have truly lived up to what I have been told. I thank you, but I think I have all I need right here," him patting his finely tailored jackets pocket, indicating he was already carrying. "I think between the three of us and a few simple weapons we can handle what awaits us."

CHAPTER 8

Present Day – Vatican City

The Vatican is considered the smallest sovereign nation in the world with its 108 acres surrounded on all sides by the capital of Italy, Rome. It is also the residence of the spiritual leadership of the Roman Catholic Church, Pope Francis. Within its stately walls are many magnificent buildings such as St Peter's Basilica, the Vatican Museums, numerous Art Galleries and what is not well known to the general public, the Vatican Vaults. The Vatican Vaults doors are sealed to all but the Pope himself and a select chosen few scholars and ranking members of the Vatican Guards. One of those few is the head of Papal Security, Stefano Gia. In his stately position he answers to no one but the Pope. It is Stefano's job to ensure nothing, absolutely nothing happens that would ever smear the Vatican; *again*. It is also his job to make sure the Vatican Vaults stay out of the press. In addition, to say as little as possible about the Vaults' existence. Over the years, the Vatican Vaults have been accused of hiding everything from Corporate and Mafia holdings to Nazi secrets. It was those Nazi secrets that were rumored to number in the billions of euros.

Of course, Vatican secrets had to be protected. And those that protect are authorized to do whatever it takes to keep them from being exposed.

Whatever it takes.

****

IT WAS JUST another typical day in Vatican City handling the usual tourist issues such as pickpockets and counterfeit ticket hawkers. Stefano Gia had better things to do with his time as he walked over to his senior assistant, Marco Ricci.

"Walk with me thru the Gardens," Stefano said. "Let us leave the mundane work to the guards to handle. We have much to talk about."

Marco had no choice but to honor the simple request, and the Vatican gardens were supposed to be beautiful this time of year, especially when they were closed to tourists.

They walked in silence past the crowds of St. Peters Square and down a narrow alley until they came to an elaborate iron gate that stood for centuries guarding its entrance. Stefano pulled an ancient key from his pocket and opened the gate to a loud squeak. "Please, after you," he said as he allowed his assistant to walk through first. "Is this your first time in the gardens?" he asked his assistant, a recent hire, him merely nodding in response. "Let's walk clock wise so I can show you some of its particulars and we can talk about a special job I have for you." For several minutes they walked in silence until Stefano spoke. "The first parts of the Vatican Gardens were created by Pope Nicholas III in the 13th century, meant to be a space for peaceful reflection."

Marco nodded. "Its beauty is stunning."

"As you will notice, over the centuries, the landscaped gardens, grassy spaces, and orchards have grown to cover nearly one-half of the Vatican's area and rival the most beautiful gardens in Italy."

They walked in silence past the formal French Garden, eyeing its many individually potted plants along its paths, containing azaleas and other lush flowers. Planted among these and in the orchard were several rare trees, including an Australian silk-oak, as well as many trees that were brought as gifts by official visitors. Perhaps the most significant of these trees is the olive tree, which was presented by the State of Israel to symbolize peaceful relations with the head of the Catholic Church.

When they reached the olive tree Stefano pulled from his shirt pocket a plain white business card with the name *Enrico Costa* printed in bold, black lettering; a local cell phone number printed under it. It had been several months since Enrico last performed a favor for Stefano. Truth was, Stefano was hoping to never have to use him again. He even went as far as promising His Holiness he would dispose of the card and never speak of the man again. However, this was an urgent situation and urgent situations required someone like Enrico Costa. "I told you earlier that I have a very special job for you," he said. "It's one where, due to my position, I cannot be involved. You understand don't you?"

"I understand that you are close to his Holiness and sometimes you have to off-load some of your more *delicate work.*"

Stefano grinned at the naïve man. "Yes, that's correct," he said. He then handed the business card to his assistant. "Call that number on the card and ask for Enrico Costa. When you reach him, inform him Stefano has a *ghost job involving the Amber Room* for him. It's to be his last and he will be well-compensated."

Marco had a puzzled look on his face as he eyed the business card.

Stefano smiled at his middle-aged assistant. "You have nothing to worry about. Just tell him exactly what I told you. *Exactly*, mind you. The man is a professional. He will know what to do."

Marco simply nodded as his expression turned to one of apprehension.

"If you think you are not up to such a simple task, I can always arrange for someone else to do it."

Marco didn't want to jeopardize his new position. "No, sir," Marco said. "I can handle it."

"Good," said Stefano. "Like I said, it's nothing for you to worry about. You are just following my orders."

And that was *precisely* what Marco was worried about.

****

THE FARM RUSSO was set amongst the rolling green hills of Arquata and Colcimino, in the Montefalco area of Umbria, an area famous for its fine Italian red wines. It covered an impressive area of about 40 hectares of land with 30 dedicated to vineyards and 10 to olive groves, famous since roman times for its high quality olive oil and wine. The winery itself was set in an old convent of the Friars Celestine, built on Roman ruins thousands of years old. Sometimes it felt like the house was also a thousand years old due to its constant need of work, and a lot of money for its upkeep. *A lot of money.*

A solitary hunched figure walked in from yet another early morning of tending his vines and planting some new ones. Never enough time in the day to accomplish everything that had to be done. There was always work to do.

Enrico Costa swatted away the gnats that seemed to follow him everywhere. His long, slender nose was set above a full crooked mouth where a cigarette dangled from its corner. The perpetually tanned Enrico had retired to his farm only three years ago. He took the money and ran so to say. After many years of working for some really unsavory people he decided it was time to get out while he still was alive. He realized it was only a matter of time before his employers would find a way to get him killed in one of their many schemes. Approaching 62 years of age, he decided it best to just walk away. His wife had died of cancer several years before and he decided enough was enough.

As he walked towards the farms bottling room one of his employees ran over to hand him a cell phone. "Signore, you have a call from the Vatican," he said excitedly.

Enrico nodded politely to the man before taking the phone. He composed himself for a few seconds. H knew they only called when they needed something of importance. "This is Enrico," he said confidently but in a low tone. "How may I be of assistance to you this time?"

The middle-aged assistant identified himself before repeating exactly what his boss had said, placing the emphasis on the term '*Ghost work involving the Amber Room.*' He waited for Enrico to confirm the message but heard no reply.

Enrico stood staring at the phone for several seconds. He then began to perspire. His hands suddenly became clammy. He knew what he had to do. Only one person knew the code: the head of Papal security.

"Did you hear me, Enrico? "Ghost Work," the assistant repeated himself in a more forceful voice.

"I heard you the first time you little snot," he replied angrily into the phone. He looked to his watch. "Give me a few hours to get ready and I will be at the usual location around five this afternoon. Have everything ready to go."

After he hung up, he felt the hairs on his neck suddenly rise.

Enrico had a bad feeling about this job.

CHAPTER 9

October 1944: St. Joseph's Church, Königsberg

Perluci was running out of time. The Russians were getting closer by the day. It was now or never if he were to make his move. In the first week of October Perluci approached a local carpenter who performed odd jobs around the Church. He led the carpenter down to the Church's basement and shown him the wooden crates that contained the Amber Room. He asked the carpenter if he could construct identical crates, careful to include all markings down to a spray painted German eagle on each. The carpenter informed him that the job was a simple tasking; all he required to start the job was money to pay for the wood. Perluci handed him 50 Marks on the spot. He then informed him that the job was a secret project; no one was to know what he was doing. The carpenter, in dire need of money due to the war-time food shortages striking the city, readily agreed.

In three days' time the carpenter returned in his truck and approached Perluci, his work now complete. Perluci had the carpenter move the crates under the cover of darkness to the church's basement and its rear storage room. Even though he was in his early sixties he was a bull of a man.

When the carpenter had completed his task, Perluci met him in the church's graveyard for payment. "I hope you stuck to our agreement," he inquired of the carpenter, the weight of his words hung in the night air.

"Of course, Father," he replied meekly. "You said the work was secret; mention it to no one. I didn't even inform my wife. She even assumed I had a girlfriend due to the late nights I have spent at my shop."

Perluci grinned at the man's honesty. He reached under his cassock and extracted a pistol with a silencer already attached, leveling the pistol at the carpenters head. "You are a good man, but you know I can't have any loose ends."

"But you are a priest!" the carpenter replied, his voice trembling. "You cannot commit murder!"

"I have grave news for you, my son. I'm not really a priest." Two soft pings escaped from the pistol, the carpenter falling to the ground dead beside a freshly dug grave. Perluci used his foot to shove the body into the grave. "Never trust anyone," he said aloud, thrusting a handful of German Marks onto the dead body. "And you can't say I never paid you."

CHAPTER 10

Present Day – Castletownbere, Ireland

Jim held open the bar door for Nora and Eian as they stepped into a familiar place, MacCarthy's Pub and Grocery. It was only six weeks or so since they last visited to celebrate the life of their friend, Dan Flaherty with an *Irish Wake*. Amazingly, the place was lively for the middle of the afternoon on a weekday.

In the rugged areas of Ireland where the population is sparse, many businesses pull double duty: restaurant and butcher shop; drapery and photo shop; bar and grocery, and such.

The front half being a grocers shop with seats for drinkers; the back half, a bar with groceries. To their left, a fridge full of milk, eggs, cheese, butter and bottles of white

THE VATICAN'S FINAL SECRET by FRANCIS JOSEPH SMITH

wine. Behind the bar stood grocery shelves lined with cans of corn, spam, and ketchup.

Jim loved the look of the old time Irish Pub as they bellied up to the bar, looking to the stocked shelves of canned goods that occupied shelves behind the dark wood mahogany bar. To his left he saw an old-fashioned, stain glassed and mahogany wood *'snug'*: a private little area in the front of the bar for a time when it was frowned upon for women to be in a bar, the parish priest for his daily whisky, or maybe lovers for a rendezvous.

Jim indicated for Eian and Nora to go sit in the snug while he went to the bar to grab them a few pints of Guinness. While at the bar waiting for his pints to finish he queried the bartender, a middle-aged woman with a constant smile upon her face, if she knew of a Shannon Flaherty. Jim lied and said they were friends and wanted to get in touch with her. The bartender pondered the question for a few minutes before she knocked on the wood bar in response. "She is the young lass who inherited her mom's farm just outside of town. Shame, the mom died of cancer so quickly. What I heard was the daughter returned from Dublin to run the place. Don't see much of her. She is busy with the farm seven days a week. Sheep's Hollow Farm is the name of the place." She provided him directions the old fashioned way: on back of a cocktail napkin.

Jim returned to the table with the three Guinness in tow. He placed the beers on the table before he handed the napkin to Nora. "Got the directions to the farm where Shannon lives."

Nora eyed the napkin, holding it up as a smile creased her face. "You couldn't simply plug the address into your iPhone?" She said.

"Things are a little different around here," he replied. "A little slower and more laid back."

Nora knew Jim to be slightly technology deficient and took it all in stride. She looked at the napkin more closely. "It looks like we could walk to the place from here," she said.

"Don't be fooled, my dear," replied Jim. "Everything around here is just down the road, or just a wee walk. From what the bartender said, it's close to ¾ of a mile outside of town just off the main road.

Eian raised his glass. "To finding another lost relative and hopefully the other half of the clue to the Amber Room."

Jim and Nora followed suit.

Eian downed half his beer before he placed the glass on the table in front of him. He appeared to be in a remarkable mood since landing in his homeland. "What do you say we stay in town for the night and see her in the morning? We could sample some of the local beverages."

This was one of those *oh hell* moments, one where you know what's going to happen if you do, damned if you don't.

"I guess we could do that," replied Dan, turning to Nora for her agreement.

"Only if we can go visit Dan's grave in the morning," said Nora. "Bring him some fresh flowers."

"How could I not agree to such a simple request?" said Jim.

"You married a real winner, Jim," said Eian.

The bartender approached with a tray of shot glasses, each full of Jamison whiskey. "Its compliments of the gent over in the corner. Says last time you were here you bought the same for him."

Dan looked behind the bartender to see an older man in a shabby tweed sports coat and an Irish flat cap raise his glass in toast to him.

"*It's going to be one of those nights,*" he said to Nora and Eian.

CHAPTER 11

Present Day – La Porta Hotel; Rome, Italy

Squeezed in between a tour operator and a supplier of
cheap tourist trinkets, the La Porta hotel was not so much a
hotel as it was a doorway with a non-descript sign hung
above it that announced its presence. Tourists tended to shy
away from the worn door, seemingly always locked. As
they should since it was a front for the Vatican's
Intelligence Agency, located technically in Rome, just
outside The Vatican's south entrance. Perfect for them to
operate as a drop for people like Enrico. The hotels location
also enabled The Vatican to keep its hands clean and assign
its dirty work and honestly state that no criminal activity
was allowed on Vatican premises'.

Enrico Costa walked up to the front door,
depressing its circular brass door bell, an electronic buzzing
sound soon followed, the door opening just enough for

Enrico to push it the remaining distance. Enrico smiled at the well-dressed clerk who stood behind the desk. He knew the routine; with his passport in hand, he casually laid it on the counter, opened to his photo for the clerk to see whom he was dealing with.

The clerk nodded as he took Enrico's passport and held it down on an electronic scanner, waiting until the passport was verified via a loud audible click. The clerk then pointed to a retina scanner positioned on top of the counter. "Please stare into the scanner, Mr. Costa. It will only take a few seconds, Sir." Once the scanners screen turned green the clerk motioned Enrico to stand to the side. After several seconds' information flooded the clerks screen, all confirming Enrico's status. "Welcome back, Sir," the clerk beamed upon seeing he had a true celebrity staying with them. "Your boss was already here. He deposited a bag in your room."

And so it begins.

CHAPTER 12

Present Day – La Porta Hotel – Rome, Italy

Enrico opened the door to his room, poking his head in.
The room looked rather *tired*. As he stepped into the room
he noticed the carpet was worn in several spots and the
twin bed had a threadbare blanket covering its length.
Beside the bed stood a simple wooden nightstand, on its top
a lamp struggled to provide enough light for the room.
Enrico shook his head at the dump. Luckily for him it was
just a retrieval location. He moved over to the window,
pushing back the curtains to try to gain some extra light.
Unfortunately for him the window curtains looked to be
about as old as the building with numerous holes to match.
He added several more as he slid them to one side. Now he
had a good view of the mold surrounding the window
frame.

He removed a handkerchief from his pocket and
wiped his hands. *Did anyone actually pay to stay here?* He
thought to himself. In the corner of the room sat what he

came for: a black leather case with a large brown envelope on its top.

Enrico picked up the rather heavy envelope flipping it over to verify its elaborate Vatican wax seal. He stared at the seal for several seconds pondering his next move. He realized once he opened the envelope there was no turning back. However, if he changed his mind and didn't follow through they would kill him just the same. Did he have a choice? He ripped open the envelope and emptied its contents on the bed; out fell two bundles of euros and a pack of matches. He then removed and read the customary letter for his intended target. After several minutes he took the letter and the matches and walked over to the bathroom sink. He lit a match, followed by the letter, dropping the burning letter into the sink. After several seconds there was nothing but black ash.

Enrico returned to the black leather case, one about the size of old fashioned pilots map case, opening it up. Inside, in pieces, was a modified 7.62 TKIV 85 bolt-action sniper rifle, the one preferred by the Finnish Defense Force and most old-school snipers like himself. Little kick back, and good out to 600 meters. He lifted the weapon, piece by piece, screwing each piece together to check for proper fit. Satisfied, he repeated the process in reverse, placing it back in the case, piece by piece. He then reached over to the room's old style black phone and, using the rotary dial, called the front desk. When the front desk clerk picked up, Enrico said: "You know who this is, correct?"

The clerk responded affirmatively.

"Good. First, arrange a car for me. Secondly, inform your boss to get the jet ready for lift off in one hour."

"I will do as you say, sir," replied the clerk.

"And arrange for some sandwiches and coffee to be delivered to the plane," he said, looking around at the rooms surroundings. *"From a caterer, not the hotel kitchen."*

As per his instructions in the letter, Enrico was heading off to eliminate his target: destination Ireland.

CHAPTER 13

Present Day - Shannon, Ireland

Enrico's flight was a lengthy five hours from Rome. However, they were a luxurious five hours. Pampered the whole way on an Aircraft Charter Services Gulfstream 550 chartered for him by the Vatican. He usually travelled via commercial airlines, but with the sniper weapon he was carrying and its accompanying ammunition, he required a more *private* space. Thank God for the EU and its open border policies.

Upon stepping down from the aircraft Enrico was greeted by Liam Toole, a Vatican operative placed in the hinterlands of Ireland for just this purpose. At six foot five, 275 pounds, Liam stood out from his fellow compatriots. He looked more like an American Football lineman. His crooked nose attested to his boxing days at Trinity College. His looks and stature made it rather hard for him to blend in unnoticed so he was used more in an administrative capacity, providing the logistics and such.

"Welcome to Ireland," said Liam enthusiastically, firmly shaking Enrico's hand. "As they say over here, '*A hundred thousand welcomes to you.*'"

Enrico nodded. He was impatient and ready to get on with his job. "Did you hire me a car?" He said impatiently.

"Yes, sir," Liam replied. "I also arranged for a hotel room near the job site. And, as per your instructions, I also loaded your car with some necessities for your room."

Liam offered the car keys to Enrico. "Everything you need is in this envelope."

Enrico nodded his thanks. "I may also need your help at a moment's notice. No questions asked."

"Here is my number," he replied. "I am available to you 24/7, sir." He handed him his business card.

Enrico held up the business card as he entered the driver's side of the rental car. "Make sure that you are," he said rather ominously before he drove off.

CHAPTER 14

Present Day

One km west of Castletownbere, Ireland

The Ford Opel had traveled almost a kilometer to the west of Castletownbere. The cars two occupants were there to visit the grave of their one time partner, Dan Flaherty.

A sign on the right-hand side of the desolate road proudly proclaimed in Celtic: *Cill Achadh an Eanaigh*, or Glebe Graveyard. Jim parked on the side of the road and exited the car. He walked around to the passenger side of the car to open the door, allowing Nora to exit with a smile gracing her face. "Thank-you, sir," she said playfully, as he grabbed her hand to help her exit the vehicle. They entered a small byway that meandered a couple of hundred years into the past over the course of the 200 meters it took to reach the cemetery. The pathway was little more than slightly trampled grass, easily mistaken for a path left by the many grazing sheep who inhabited the area.

A small wooden gate announced the entrance to the cemetery. The gate had an arch clad in overgrown Ivy. As they pushed open the gate it was if stepping back in time. Looking to the left and right they noticed that some of the inhabitants of this little graveyard had been interred there since the 1700s. The place was peaceful and overgrown in places with trailing ivy and winding creepers. Some of the grave markers were so old they were little more than plain stones resting their worn heads on the green grass.

Some of the markers were clustered together, leaning towards each other as if sharing secrets or stories.

Jim and Nora looked at the many names on the stones: O'Connell, O'Sullivan, Mealy, Murphy, McCarthy. Many of the surnames were those of local families who continue to live in the same area as their families' generations had before them. Having visited the cemetery with Nora only six weeks ago, Jim knew exactly where Dan was buried as he walked just beyond the overgrown church ruins, over by the north-west wall of the cemetery.

"There he is," said Jim as he pointed over to the grave. "It's one of the few new graves to be dug in here for years." Dan was the latest, with another just beside him, buried the year before. They walked the 20 meters or so to the grave. Jim pulled two shot glasses and a small bottle of Jamison Irish Whisky from his jackets pocket as he placed them on top of the tombstone. He then took his place beside Nora.

"It's so beautiful here, Jim," she said as she gazed lazily at the overgrown cemetery.

"And peaceful," he replied in-turn. "Maybe we should buy a place in town."

THE VATICAN'S FINAL SECRET by FRANCIS JOSEPH SMITH

Nora nodded. "I agree. A small place that we can escape from the summer heat of the Florida Keys."

They had been celebrating the night before at one of the local pubs in town, buying drinks for all the locals, toasting to their friend, Dan Flaherty. "He would have enjoyed last night. Eian still is, passed out at one of the tables," making reference to their other partner and pilot, Eian Murphy.

They both laughed aloud at the thought of Eian singing drunken karaoke at 2 am.

Jim reached down for the bottle and proceeded to pour a shot of Jamison into each glass before he poured the remainder of the bottle onto Dan's grave. When the bottle was empty they raised their glasses in a toast to Dan, consuming the glasses contents.

Jim said aloud: "To our friend and partner in crime, Daniel Flaherty."

He placed the empty bottle by the headstone along with his and Nora's glass. "He'll like this," Jim said, a tear rolling down his cheek. He then placed a hand on his friend's grave. "I'll be back often, my friend," making a sign of the cross as he rose.

Nora smiled as she placed a decorative bouquet of flowers on the grave of Dan, resting them against the headstone next to the empty bottle. "He was a lovely man."

Nora grabbed his arm, tucking it under her own, as she led him to the graveyards exit. "He was a true gentleman."

Arm in arm they strolled down the byway.

As they approached their rental car Jim laughed aloud once more as he turned to face Nora. "I think we better get back to collect Eian," he said, "before he starts drinking again."

Nora smiled wide. "That's the last thing we need."

A hint of sunlight reflecting off glass or possibly stainless steel caught Jim's attention.

"What's the matter?" asked Nora, seeing a look of seriousness return to Jim's face, amazed at how the former Navy SEAL could shift gears so easily.

"I think we're being watched," he said. "Just act normal."

CHAPTER 15

Present Day - MacCarthy's Bar and Grocery, Castletownbere, Ireland

Eian Murphy lifted his head from the small wooden table where it had been resting comfortably since passing out at 4 am, now feeling a bit woozy from his previous night's activities. He looked about his surroundings, puzzled for a moment or two before he gathered his wits about him. "How the hell did I wind up in a damn grocery store?"

"How are you feeling this morning, lad?" queried the 40ish wisp of a barmaid as she wiped off the table where he sat. "They said to just let you sleep it off."

Eian shook his head. "Did a damn truck run over me?" he replied in an Irish accent now thicker since he had landed in his native Ireland.

The barmaid shook her head and laughed aloud as she took a tray of dirty beer glasses to the kitchen. "Oh, aren't you the funny one."

The bartender/grocery clerk stood behind the counter shaking his baldhead. "Next time drink some water with your whiskey, young man," wisely imparting the wisdom gained of his 45 years behind the bar. "No hangover. Guaranteed." With many pubs in Ireland being taken over by corporations, it was good to see one that was still owner-operated, by a real publican.

"Okay, Pops," replied Eian. "Right now I just need some peace and quiet."

The bartender smiled. "You young pups could learn a thing or two from us old timers."

Eian flashed him a smile. "My Dad said the same thing to me when I was seventeen and look where it got me."

A sudden screech of tires followed quickly by the sound of slamming car doors originating from just outside the bars front door; then the sight of two men bursting through the door brandishing 9mm's. One was quick to point his weapon at the bartender. "It will be your last if you make a move," he said in a Belfast accent. "Don't do it, back away from behind the bar and come out where I can see you better."

The second man pointed his weapon directly at Eian. "I see you are awake from your little sleep," he said in the same accent as his partner. "Now stand up and come with us," he said, motioning with his weapon towards the door.

Eian looked at each before responding. 'What's this all about boys?" He said with a hint of sarcasm. I thought the IRA was dead and gone? Maybe you boys in the rugged west didn't get the word yet?"

The man replied by raising the gun above his head and firing a single shot into the tin plated ceiling. "Get your ass up and out the door. Now!"

"You have such a wonderful vocabulary," Eian replied sarcastically. He nodded before slowly rising up from his chair, shaking his head, in effect laughing at the man. "Your Mum must be proud of the profession you have taken up."

Hassan Talif walked in just as Eian was rising from his chair. Hassan nodded to his IRA henchmen then focused on Eian. "Good morning, Mr. Eian Murphy," he said, smiling. "You are Eian Murphy, the pilot? Correct?"

Eian smiled in return. "You have me at a disadvantage, sir."

"Yes, of course. So sorry. Allow me to introduce myself. I am Hassan Talif," he bowed slightly as he said his introduction. "We had hoped to find both you and your friends, James Dieter and his new bride, Nora. Where are they?" inquired Hassan as he walked over to where Eian now stood, maneuvering to within inches of his face.

"Do you honestly think I would tell you if I knew?" Eian shot back with some satisfaction. "And I just woke up a few minutes ago. Ask any of the kind people here."

The bartender spoke up. "I can vouch for the man. He just woke up. The man was drinking heavy last night."

Hassan hastily pulled a 9mm from his waistband as he turned and fired a single shot at the bartender, the bullet striking him in the chest just above his heart, driving him back into a rack of wine bottles, him falling to the floor. "I wasn't talking to you," he replied to the now dead man.

The waitress screamed at the sight of the bartender lying dead on the floor, blood pooling about him.

Hassan turned to smile at Eian. "I mean business, Mr. Murphy. The sooner you figure this out the sooner this town resumes its typical day time activities."

Eian looked to the dead bartender, then to Hassan, before replying in a steady tone, anger mounting in his voice. "I already told you, I don't know a thing. Honestly. Now leave these good people alone. If it's me you want, then do it already. Shoot me."

Hassan once again raised his weapon before nonchalantly firing a single bullet at the waitress, the bullet hitting her square in the chest, her falling dead to the floor.

Eian's eyes went wide. "Jesus Christ! You're a damn lunatic!"

Hassan nodded to one of his men. The man walked out the door, motioning to a boy of about 12 or 13 who was unfortunate enough to be riding his bike in the wrong place at the wrong time. He forcefully hauled the boy off his bike, the boy kicking and screaming as he did, before dragging him into the bar. The man then deposited the boy on the floor in front of Hassan where he grabbed the boy around the neck with his free hand. In his other hand he held his 9mm, now pressed to the boy's temple. "Quiet boy. No harm will come to you if our friend here," he pointed over to Eian with his weapon, "answers my questions."

Eian could see where this was going. None of it good. "Okay, okay. I'll talk. You don't have to kill the whole damn town. Let the boy go and I'll tell you what you want to know."

Hassan smiled as he placed the 9mm back into his waistband. "So quick to change your mind?" he replied before letting the boy go. The boy took one look at Hassan, then Eian, tears welling in his eye before he sprinted out the front door.

"I don't like to kill children, Mr. Murphy, but if I have to."

"Yes, I know your type. Hezbollah. Dealt with your kind many times. Should have smelled you coming but the wind is blowing out to sea today."

Hassan laughed aloud. "And that is the reason why I am here. Here in this rainy, cloudy, country of yours. I would like to go home as soon as possible. And you can help me achieve this by telling me where your friends are."

Eian looked first to the two IRA henchmen, then to their boss, Hassan. He smiled wide. "They went fishing," he said, his tone mocking them.

Hassan withdrew his pistol once more before roughly slamming its butt into Eian's chin, him falling to the floor in obvious pain. Hasson then brought the pistol to bear on Eian as he lay sprawled on the floor. "I don't think you get the true meaning of the word death."

"Trust me, I do," replied Eian as he used his shirts sleeve to wipe the blood from his chin. "I can even spell it. D-E-A-T-H. And one way or another, it's coming towards you."

Hassan smiled. "I like this man. Now get him into the car."

CHAPTER 16

Present Day - MI-6 HQ; River House – London

Its headquarters sat on the banks of the River Thames by Vauxhall Bridge, and said to resemble a futuristic prison in some outer space movie. To others, it was just a plain old eyesore on historical London. Britain's Secret Intelligence Service (SIS), commonly identified as MI6 (Military Intelligence, Section 6), didn't really care what people thought about its *concrete monstrosity*. They had a job to provide its government with much valued foreign intelligence whether it was from a doghouse or a prison.

The MI-6 employees who worked in *"the monstrosity"* suffered from what the British commonly referred to as the "coal miner effect." Workers who entered their workspaces before the sun rose and left after it had already set. One such employee who suffered from the "effect" was Roscoe Hopkins: tall and gangly, pale skin the sun had rarely kissed, bald as a cue, cauliflower ears from his amateur boxing days.

His office lacked windows due to his boss' level of importance. Another measure put into place in a constant effort to improve security. This prevented any sort of eavesdropping or assassination attempts from the street level, a mere nine floors below.

Employed as an executive assistant to Sir Robert John, Director of MI-6, Hopkins was intimately associated with most of the top-secret operations and events that transpired not only in the United Kingdom, but also worldwide. Even the Prime Minister was not aware of most active operations.

Hopkins busily arranged the morning's messages and newspaper clippings. The clippings were courtesy of the morning duty officer. Hopkins arranged them by operational theater, just the way his boss preferred: Europe, the Americas, and so on.

He walked up to Sir Robert's office, door still open, knocking lightly to announce his presence, waiting until his director had looked up from his morning newspaper before entering.

"Sir Robert, sorry to bother you, but you have a red message," Hopkins said. He walked over and laid the folder on Sir Robert's desk. "I took a peek, sir. Evidently, one of our communication stations outside of Cheltenham intercepted a message indicating something brewing in Ireland."

Sir Robert John provided Roscoe Hopkins "carte blanche" on reading message traffic, allowing him to review all messages no matter what level stamp, thus weeding out all of the unnecessary and trivial traffic before reaching his desk. Sir Robert leaned back in his chair, wondering what could possibly make his day even more interesting. Most found Sir Robert to be a gentleman's gentleman: head shaven bald, tall and fit, ruggedly handsome to most, along with a touch of old English charm and an elegance long forgotten. He was well respected in the circles he moved, both professionally and personally. Sir Robert had recently celebrated his forty-third year with MI-6, one of the old-timers recruited out of Oxford University by the legendary Sir Newton Clive, former head of the MI-6 Overseas branch, long since departed.

After readily accepting Sir Clive's rather generous offer for employment, he was quickly put to work. First it was the tedious mission of breaking codes or ciphers, as they were then known, before being sent to a posting at the new communications complex outside Cheltenham. After ten years of tedious deskwork duty, he badgered his boss enough to receive an assignment to work in the former West Germany. Within months, he was able to penetrate the "Iron Curtain," eventually doing so on eleven separate missions. Within two years, he even managed to *turn* an East German Army General whom he personally escorted across the border. This led to a real intelligence coup for the western powers. For that distinction, he received the honorary title of "Sir" by the Queen. Moving up rapidly through the ranks, he naturally assumed the directorship of MI-6 when the sitting director retired several years before.

"The Hezbollah sent out the equivalent of an encrypted all-points bulletin on James Dieter, which we easily intercepted and broke at Cheltenham," Hopkins replied efficiently, his boss not having to search for information. Hezbollah being a Shi'a Islamist militant group and political party based in Lebanon. "They say he may be in Ireland. You remember him, Sir Robert: He was a friend of Daniel Flaherty, the last of the IRA henchmen."

Sir Robert nodded in recollection. "Yes, I remember Flaherty. But from what I recall, Flaherty died in Lebanon going after that Martin Bormann treasure," he said, referring to the Nazi gold secreted after WWII by Bormann.

"Yes, sir," replied Hopkins. "Dieter had him buried in Ireland and he and his wife are evidently over there now with the intention of visiting his grave."

Sir Robert looked up to Hopkins. "Didn't I read somewhere that Dieter and Flaherty assisted the Israelis in killing Sheik Hassan Nasrallah."

Hopkins nodded. "Yes, sir. It seems they placed blame on Dieter for the Sheik and his top lieutenant's death from a missile strike. We both know the Israelis and the Americans performed the actual deed and that Dieter was just a patsy. But that seems to be the reason they want James Dieter dead." He placed a second red folder. "And this one caught me by surprise. A real shocker. The Vatican evidently is after Dieter for putting the spotlight on their WWII activities."

Sir Robert took a moment to gaze at a portrait of Winston Churchill that hung above his conference table. He looked to be in deep thought before he abruptly came alive, turning to face Hopkins. "Well we are not going to let it happen. I want you to see who we have operational in the area that can provide the Dieter's with some assistance."

Hopkins nodded to his boss before placing a printout on his desk. "I anticipated your request and took

THE VATICAN'S FINAL SECRET by FRANCIS JOSEPH SMITH

the liberty of pulling the records on the only two operatives known to be in that area."

Sir Robert looked up and smiled at Hopkins. "It's almost as if you can read my mind and anticipate my every move. Sometimes you are worse than my damn wife," he said. "Contact them and put a *at their discretion* label on the handling of this operation. I want you to personally follow up on this and keep me abreast of the situation."

Hopkins realized all too well what a *at their discretion* label meant: Sir Robert just signed a death warrant for those trailing Dieter and his wife.

CHAPTER 17

Present Day - One km west of Castletownbere, Ireland

A hundred meters further down the road from the Glebe Graveyard, under the cover of a row of overgrown hedges, a man in a finely tailored suit adjusted his Swiss made binoculars, focusing in on Jim and Nora as they exited the graveyard and approached their rental car.

There was nothing separating them but rugged mountains to the left, the jagged coast to the right and the road that ran in the center. Not even a building was in site, just stone walls built from the one crop every Irish farm seemed to have in abundance: rocks.

Satisfied it was indeed his target the man placed his binoculars on top of the stone wall in front of him, picking up his cell phone and after several seconds was connected to his boss. "They appear to be on their way back," he said in a crisp English accent. "Should I stay with them?"

THE VATICAN'S FINAL SECRET by FRANCIS JOSEPH SMITH

The voice on the other end asked him to confirm the identities of his subjects, having been duped more than once in their surveillance over the course of the past several months.

The man followed up with the simple request as he picked up his binoculars once more and focused in on their last position. "What the?" he said to himself, now only observing the woman as she entered the driver's side of the car. "Where's my target?" In addition, to make it even more puzzling, the woman seemed to be smiling in his general direction. He moved the binoculars from side-to-side as he searched in vain for Jim. *Did he return to the graveyard for something?* He thought to himself. After 10 seconds or so the car was being driven down the road in his direction. He focused the binoculars at the graveyards exit then to the car itself to see if Jim was in the passenger seat. "Where….," he muttered to himself, "*did the man go?*"

As Nora drove the car slowly past the man's position, an arm reached around his neck, then a boney knee in his back, in effect choking him, causing him to drop the binoculars to the ground as struggled with his powerful assailant. It was a short struggle, the SEAL headlock worked every time. In a matter of seconds, he passed out.

When he awoke, Jim had the man on his stomach, hands behind his back. Nora held the man's Walther PPK.

"Sorry about dirtying your suit," Jim said sarcastically. "Would you care to tell me who you're working for?" With his right hand Jim forced the man's elbows up towards the back of his head, with his left hand he yanked the man's hair back.

"Let me go you bastard," the man screamed in obvious pain.

Jim pushed the man's elbows further up his back.

The man screamed aloud once more, before wisely choosing to respond: "I work for Sir Robert John, Director of MI-6," he said in obvious agony. Jim paused for a split second, all too familiar with the head of Britain's Secret Intelligence Agency. He released his grip on the man. "I should have recognized the hand-tailored suit and the standard issue Walther PPK," Jim replied as he extended his hand to help pull the man up and off the ground.

The man nodded his thanks. "Thomas Wraith," he said.

"Good to know you, Mr. Wraith," replied Jim. "Of course you already know who we are so I won't have to introduce you to my wife.

Nora nodded as she handed him back his weapon. "I believe this is yours," she said with a smirk gracing her face.

"I should have expected as much from MI-6," said Jim.

The MI-6 Agent retrieved his Walther PPK from Nora. "Yes, I was informed you would be traveling with a very attractive women who also won a Pulitzer Prize," he said, winking at Nora.

"And intelligent," she replied. "There are so few of us, beautiful *and* intelligent."

Jim looked to the MI-6 Agent. "See what I have to deal with?"

"From where I am standing, you are a very lucky man, sir."

Nora eyed Jim with a smile on her face. "Mr. Dieter, I would say you have some competition."

Jim ignored her. "So, Thomas Wraith," he said, "I would guess you are going to fill us in on why you were spying on us?"

"Yes, how rude of me. Sir Robert John asked me to keep an eye on the two of you due to some traffic we picked up from Hezbollah. And, of all places the Vatican. It seems both organizations have some people looking to eliminate you."

Jim looked to Nora and then back to the MI-6 agent. "You have got to be kidding me? The Hezbollah *and* the Vatican?"

Nora laughed aloud. "James Dieter I can't take you anywhere where you don't piss people off, can I?"

The agent continued: "They may already be in Ireland as we speak."

"Hezbollah maybe because he helped remove one or two of their people. But the Vatican?" Jim repeated.

"From what I have been told," the agent said, "The Vatican blames you for a multitude of things. I think number one on the list is something about the Amber Room…," his voice tapered off as he suddenly fell to the ground.

"What the hell?" said Jim upon eyeing blood flowing freely from a hole in the man's head the size of a dime. "Cover! Sniper!" he yelled, abruptly leaping up from his prone position to push Nora behind a stone wall for cover.

"I think we pissed somebody off," said Nora to Jim who was now laying on her back in a shielding position.

"You think?" was his reply.

"Never a dull moment with you, James Dieter. Is this the kind of excitement I can expect for the rest of our marriage?"

Nora couldn't see him smile as he responded. "You have to admit, I really know how to show a girl a good time. *But to answer your question: yeah, pretty much.*"

CHAPTER 18

January 1945: St. Joseph's Church, Königsberg

The sound of heavy trucks, their diesel engines belching heavy black smoke, signaled the arrival of Dr. Alfred Rohde, this the first Saturday morning after the Allied Bombing raid that destroyed the Castle. Perluci knew this day would come and had anticipated his arrival. If not to remove the treasure secreted in the church's basement, than to at least check on its condition.

Perluci was busily tending to his winter garden box on the side of the church that received the most amount of sunshine. He wiped his brow with a handkerchief upon seeing the two trucks as they hissed to a stop by the church's basement entrance, their black crosses painted upon their door announcing where their allegiance lay.

Perluci nodded to Rohde as he stepped down from the trucks passenger cab. At the same time four German soldiers exited from the rear of each truck, taking their place behind Rohde. "Something wrong?" asked Perluci as he placed his handkerchief back into his pocket.

Rohde simply smiled in return as he pointed to the church's basement door. "Could you please open this? We are removing our valuables to a much safer location before the British or American bombers decide to strike again."

Perluci had prayed for this moment. He had wanted the crates and the Germans out of the Church. "That will not be a problem, Dr. Rohde," he said, pulling a ring of keys from his pocket. "Always glad to be of assistance," he lied as he fumbled with three keys before the fourth opened the door.

Rohde roughly pushed Perluci aside before he walked down the steps to the basement, his soldiers followed closely behind. At the bottom of the steps he turned on the lights one-by-one, before the entire basement lay bathed in light. He eyed his crates appreciatively before handing a crowbar to the soldier nearest him.

Perluci had made his way to the basement in time to watch Rohde as he barked orders about which crates were to be opened for inspection. At first, the soldier was set to open one of the larger crates, but Rohde turned in time to see Perluci mopping his brow, a worried expression upon his face. Something wasn't right, he thought to himself. Rohde smiled at Perluci before pointing to the two smallest crates that lay just to the rear.

Perluci knew he didn't stand a chance if he had to turn and run. One of the soldiers would merely cut him down in a hail of gunfire in a matter of seconds.

Rohde motioned for one of the soldiers to stand behind Perluci. "If he moves, shoot him," he said.

The soldier withdrew his pistol, pointing it at the base of Perluci's back.

Rohde turned his attention to the soldier with the crow bar. "Stop! He yelled. "I changed my mind. Open the two crates to the right."

Perluci took a deep breath.

The soldier moved to the crates to the right, sliding the crowbar under the crates wooden lid, pushing the crowbar down, the nails screeching in reply. The lid slid off easy enough. The soldier searched inside the crate, before nodding to Rohde everything was secure.

"Check the next one," barked Rohde, eyeing Perluci then the second crate.

The soldier performed the same operation to the second crate. "All here, sir," said the soldier.

Rohde turned to Perluci. "My apologies but I had to be sure," he said, before signaling for the soldier to holster his weapon.

Perluci breathed a sigh of relief. He realized he was within seconds of death as he now watched the soldiers remove the crates from the basement to the awaiting trucks.

After 30 minutes the basement lay bare once more. All of its contents were now safely onboard the trucks. Perluci grinned as he watched Rohde drive off in a cloud of black smoke.

It was now or never, he said to himself. He had to move fast. Rohde might choose to open the open the rest of the crates or he could keep them packed up and ready to move back to Germany. Perluci couldn't take the chance. Everything was riding on the next phase of his plan.

It was time.

CHAPTER 19

Present Day - One km west of Castletownbere, Ireland

Nora looked to Jim, then to the dead body of the British MI-6 agent as he lay face up on the ground before them. She braced herself up against an ancient stonewall, piled stone-by-stone by some unknown farmer hundreds of years ago. "What have we gotten ourselves into, James Dieter?"

Jim ignored her for a few seconds as he eyed the bullets entry point on the dead agent, trying to deduce the possible direction of the shooter. Satisfied, he turned to face Nora. "You should have known when you married me that it would be one adventure after another."

Nora smiled. "I have to warn you. If this is what I can expect for the next few years of marriage, it might get a little rocky."

He pointed over to a row of tall hedges that lined the road all the way back to their car, the same path that hid his approach to the now dead MI-6 agent. "We have to get out of here and be quick about it or we will soon join our friend here."

"Don't tell me, I'm first? Right?"

Jim could only manage a meek smile in return. "Good, a volunteer," he said, patting her hand. "Now, I am going to try and place a few rounds where I think the shooter is hiding to give us a little bit of a start. Hopefully providing us the cover we need."

"James Dieter, just promise me that this won't become an everyday event with you?"

"No promises. But I did say life with me would be interesting."

"I thought that's what you would say. Shall we say on three?"

He leaned over and kissed her on the cheek. "On three it is. One, two….." On three, he raised the dead agents Walther PPK just above the rocks and took aim at an outcropping of shrubs, placing three rounds right where he would be sitting if he were a shooter. Nora quickly sprinted towards the tree line, Jim followed her several seconds later, now on her heels, both making their way towards their car.

****

ENRICO COSTA HAD been in position several hours before Nora and Jim first entered the graveyard. He

105

positioned himself 200 meters from the graveyard entrance and as fate would have it, 100 meters behind the MI-6 agent. Luckily, he had overheard Nora and Jim's intentions the night before in the crowded pub making his job all the easier. What he didn't expect was the MI-6 agent. He was the wildcard. *How many people were after these two?* Enrico thought as he now observed movement with Jim raising his weapon over the rocks; he smiled as he adjusted his scope, and then readied to take his shot. "Just a little higher," he said as if trying to coax his target. Suddenly a bullet from Jim's weapon hit the branch above his head, followed by two more impacting the ground in front of him, causing dirt to fling up and into his eyes, temporarily blinding him. "How the hell did he know my position?" he mumbled aloud as he blinked rapidly trying to clear his eyes.

"Nice move," Enrico mumbled to himself as he lay on his back in obvious discomfort. "Another time, another place. But rest assured, we will meet again."

CHAPTER 20

Present Day - Jerusalem

Benny Machaim paced the sparse confines of his office, at least by Israeli definition. As head of Mossad, the Israeli intelligences equivalent of the CIA, he could have kept the antique English furniture his predecessor had left behind or chosen new from the Department of State catalog. He chose neither; a simple gunmetal desk, small wooden conference table that sat five, and a large coffee pot was enough for him. Anything more meant extravagance. The room was adorned with two pictures hung on the wall detailing his prior exploits as a Shayetet 13 commando, an elite naval commando unit of the Israeli Navy, often compared to the U.S. Navy SEALs. Standing five foot five, he was lucky to have passed the minimum height requirements of the commando. With his barrel chest and head shaven bald he was frequently compared to the American actor, Yul Brenner.

Benny looked to his subordinate, Moshe Eisen, a young man in his thirties who had served with him since the Lebanese border wars. "Are you sure that's what he said?" he said in a low voice.

"It's possible I misunderstood, Sir. But not likely," Moshe replied. "Sir Robert John of MI-6 said a Hezbollah operative was operating in Ireland. Castletownbere to be exact. One of his agents was already missing and wondering if we could lend a hand, per say. He said it pertained to the James Dieter mission and their need to seek revenge." Moshe looked up at his boss before continuing. "As you already know, we employ a few people in the area who could help if needed."

"Okay, Moshe. It might be best to make some discreet inquires. Go through our deep cover assets in the Lebanese government. They have some pull. You can't make this happen through the old-boy network. At this level you have to make a real effort to ferret out any additional info."

Moshe nodded. "I understand. Give me some time to run this to ground." He held up a cigarette. "Mind if I smoke?"

"I thought you quit after our last little exercise in Lebanon."

"I did quit. *But since you hired me as your Deputy........*"

Benny laughed aloud in response. "I should have warned you before you took the position."

Moshe laughed in-turn, exhaling smoke as he did.

"You know," Benny said, pondering his response as he looked out his window before he turned back to look at Moshe, "there is the possibility the American CIA might get wind of this and kill the whole operation before we get involved."

Moshe smiled. "The Americans have their hands in a lot of different pies right now and probably won't even care about our little operation." He stood up to leave. "But if they do, and I think you will agree with me on this, it will be one of the last things they do."

CHAPTER 21

Present Day - One km west of Castletownbere, Ireland

Nora was first to reach the car, Jim several seconds behind. Both leaned heavily against the car trying to catch their breath. "Give me the keys," Nora said, I can drive. He dutifully pitched them to her.

Jim checked the status of his Walther PPK ammunition, seeing six bullets still left. "You have to hurry back to town to check on Eian. If this bastard is out here after us, then Eian is in as much danger as we are."

"What about you," Nora said, her voice tinged with anxiety. "You can't just stay here."

"I want you to take the car and get Eian. I can stay under the cover of the hedgerows and make sure the sniper doesn't follow you."

Nora knew better than to argue with him. "All right, James Dieter," she replied. "But don't you go and get yourself killed. I don't look good in black."

Jim smiled at her. "You look great in anything, my love. Now get out of here.

In seconds she was gone.

Jim now concentrated on the sniper. Hopefully the sniper would think they both left and would soon follow in pursuit. At least that was the plan.

Now he lay in wait.

CHAPTER 22

Present Day - One km west of Castletownbere, Ireland

Nora couldn't help to take a quick peak in her rearview mirror as she left Jim to deal with the sniper. Satisfied, she then concentrated on driving the short distance to town. Once there she could grab Eian and between the two of them get some help back to Jim.

She drove past the police station. The town's lone policeman might be of some assistance after she collected Eian. That is if he carried or had access to a weapon. She realized most of the police in Ireland had no need for one.

Nora drove to the town square and parked the car. She ran across the street to MacCarthys Pub, bursting in the door only to find Eian with a gun to his head.

"Welcome, do come in and join us," said Hassan, a smile graced his face at the unexpected appearance of Nora. "You have saved me the time of hunting you down. Please sit." He pointed to a chair next to Sims. Nora sat down and observed her surroundings.

"Don't mind the dead bodies," Hassan said, as he pointed to the bodies of the barmaid and bartender. "They chose not to listen and were rewarded with a bullet."

Nora looked to Eian. He mustered a slight smile in response.

"Where is your husband, James Dieter?" said Hassan. "If he could join our little party it would be complete."

Nora looked to Hassan with disgust in her eyes. "He's gone for the day. I don't know when he might be back. So sorry."

Hassan smacked her in the back of the head with the palm of his hand. "Watch how you speak to me."

Eian started to rise in response.

Hassan leered as he now placed his weapon to Eian's head. "I think it's time for the two of you to get up and walk out the front door and into the back seat of the car. Or would you rather join these two in their eternal slumber?" Again he pointed to the dead bartender and waitress.

Eian nodded. "No worries, I'm going," he said in a matter of fact tone.

Nora decided it best to follow Eian's lead.

Once outside Eian and Nora were roughly shoved into the back seat by one of Hassan's men, the man sitting beside them jabbed his 9mm into Eian's side. Hassan jumped into the front seat. "Head east out of town. One of our passengers in the back will kindly provide us with directions to the farmhouse of one Shannon Flaherty."

CHAPTER 23

January 1945: St. Joseph's Church, Königsberg

Perluci led four farm hands down the steps of the Church's basement and then to its back room. Each of the men had occasionally performed odd jobs around the church and were thankful for the extra pocket money the church paid them. Perluci opened the door and smiled as he viewed the wooden crates, each identical in size to the ones Dr. Rohde only moments before had loaded onto his trucks, the Nazi eagle emblazoned on each. But the crates that Perluci now viewed held the real Amber room treasures.

Perluci knew he had to sacrifice some of the treasure to hide his true intentions. The crates Dr. Rohde had loaded contained the Amber Rooms cheaper bottom Amber panels so the crates would feel weighted as though they contained all of the precious cargo. Perluci desired the top panels that contained the majority of the gold, jewels and amber. So when Dr. Rohde had his men check the contents of two random crates, they viewed legitimate pieces of the treasure; bottom panels but still pieces of the Amber Room. This enabled Perluci to retain the priceless upper panels. With a little sacrifice and maneuvering, he just helped himself to the best part of the treasure.

With the cheaper Amber Room bottom panels substituted and provided to Dr. Rohde, Perluci would only require one truck to transport what remained. This because he doubled up the panels for each crate.

The four men carefully lifted each wooden crate and carried them to the upper level. Once there, they loaded the crates onto the cargo truck Perluci had purchased on the German black market. The criminals even provided high quality forged documents for the truck. Once fully loaded and secured Perluci gave each man 50 Marks for two hours work, a very generous sum considering the monthly wage for workers was 45 Marks.

Perluci gathered the men around him. "No one speaks of what we did here," he said sternly. "Is that understood?"

Each of them nodded in understanding.

"The money I just paid you also bought your silence."

Again, each of them nodded.

"Goodnight to you," he said as he casually dismissed them.

Now it was totally up to him. Just the way he liked it.

CHAPTER 24

Present Day: Ireland

Jim peered out from his concealed spot in the hedgerows as he watched and hoped for the sniper to reappear. As he waited he noticed a red car parked no more than 200 meters further west down the road. It was partially concealed just off the road in some shrubs. *I would have picked a color that at least tried to blend in*, thought Jim as he waited for someone to appear. With nothing else in the area and no traffic to speak of, that had to be the shooters vehicle. In a matter of minutes Jim was rewarded with an image of a man ambling down the hill towards the road and the red car. He looked to be carrying something in his hands, possibly a rifle. It was hard to distinguish without a pair of binoculars. *It's got to be the sniper,* he said to himself. *There's nobody else in the area.* Jim moved closer to the road but was careful to still maintain cover behind the hedgerows. He hoped to achieve a good angle for a shot if the sniper drove by. He also didn't want to present himself as too much of a target. After a minute or so he heard the sound of an approaching car. He peered out from his spot to realize it was the red car. Jim readied himself. The car was now almost even with where Jim waited, his gun raised to where he expected the driver would be sitting.

****

MARCO LOOKED DOWN the road towards where Jim Dieter and his wife had escaped only moments ago. He was confident he would locate them at some point during the day. He sat in his rental car and placed his sniper rifle on his lap. Within seconds the rifle was professionally broken down into pieces and repacked into its case. He was disappointed that his target, Jim Dieter, had not been eliminated with his first round. Even more frustrated that he hit an unknown target. A target that he wasn't being paid to eliminate. He would have to regroup and go to his secondary location: the farm outside of town where Dan Flaherty's daughter lived. Only this time his target wouldn't get away. He placed the car in drive and started down the road towards town and where he thought the farm was located. *At least where he hoped it was located.* The bar maid at the pub provided him with directions the night before. Directions that he didn't have time to write down.

Never the less, by the end of the day Dieter would be dead.

****

JIM SAT AT the edge of the hedgerow, his gun raised. Off to his right, through a slight opening in the hedgerow, he could now see the red car as it approached. As the car got closer the driver started to speed up. Jim took this as a good sign: the sniper evidently was confident that Jim was in the car that drove off.

He kept his weapon leveled at what he anticipated would be the drivers upper torso and head location. He guessed the cars speed at around 25 kilometers as he readied his shot. Three, two, one, he mentally counted down before the car came into full view. He was able to squeeze off four shots in quick succession. The first shot hit the front quarter panel shielding the engine but his second shattered the passenger side glass and the bullet continued on to hit Marco's arm, with the next two shots hitting him in the head and neck, killing him instantly. With its driver incapacitated, the car suddenly veered off the road and slowed as it hit shrubs and undergrowth no more than 50 meters from Jim's position.

Jim immediately rose from his spot, his weapon leading the way as he approached the car, its engine still running. Upon closer inspection he could see the driver was slumped against the door. Jim wasn't taking any chances. He carefully advanced to the driver's side of the car. Not seeing any movement, he pulled up on the doors handle only to be greeted by Marco's body falling out onto the ground, shoulder first. Jim knelt down to feel a pulse, detecting a slight beat. Jim could tell from his experience that the neck and head wounds were fatal. It was only a matter of minutes before he would bleed out. The driver suddenly opened his eyes and looked to Jim. "You should be the one who is dying," he said haltingly.

"Why in the hell did you try and kill me," Jim responded, realizing he had little time to obtain any information. "Who do you work for?"

The man smiled at him before erupting into a coughing fit, blood now trickling out of his mouth. "You, bastard," he said as he looked at Jim once more. "You know who sent me, you are trying to steal the Amber Room," he spat out before he died.

Jim searched the man's pockets for any form of identification realizing if he were a true professional, he wouldn't find anything, no trace of his mission or his employer. Just when he was ready to give up, Jim noticed the outline of a tattoo on his chest. He quickly removed the man's shirt only to reveal a crude tattoo of a black orthodox cross over his right breast—the Latin words *Filiolus Humilis Servo* scrawled beneath.

God's humble servant, Dieter mumbled to himself, his Catholic upbringing betraying him. His father, Hans Dieter, had warned him years ago that he too had come across the same radical group when he was in the German Army during WWII. In the fog of combat his unit had mistakenly attacked a truck loaded with gold, SS soldiers and Vatican Guards. When his men stripped the Vatican Guards for identification they found the same crude tattoo over each of their right breasts, *Filiolus Humilis Servo*. His father later established that the SS were moving gold out of Yugoslavia under the auspices of the Vatican to the safety of the Vatican Bank.

So to Jim there was only one obvious choice, the sniper was sent to kill him by *The Vatican.*

They were aware he was after the Amber Room.

****

JIM DRAGGED MARCO'S body away from the car and tossed it aside like a sack of potatoes. He had to hurry. He had to catch up with Nora and make sure she and Eian were safe. He was concerned that Marco might not be operating alone.

Jim jumped in the still running car and backed out of the shrubbery that lined the road, in seconds he was speeding off to town.

He had no idea that in less than fifteen minutes his whole world would forever change.

CHAPTER 25

Present Day - One km east of Castletownbere, Ireland

Eian and Nora sat tied up in the backseat with Berk Logan who had a gun in Eian's side. Hassan sat comfortably in the front as Sims navigated the winding back roads to Shannon's farm courtesy of Eian who was providing him with the directions. *Or being forced to.* Hassan had already warned him, if he lied or tried to misdirect them, he was a dead man.

"It's just up the road here," said Eian. "Sheep's Hollow Farm. At least that is where it's supposed to be. We haven't visited her yet to tell her the news." Eian was speaking of the news of her father's death. That was if the mother had even spoke of Dan Flaherty.

"Turn here," instructed Hassan, as he pointed left down yet another dirt road. "Let's not alert our target to our presence by passing in front."

Sims turned off as ordered. He continued to drive for another 100 meters until Hassan pointed to an area that had shoulder high bushes, just enough to hide the car from the road.

"Park in there," said Hassan.

Sims maneuvered the car so it couldn't be seen from the road.

"This is an excellent location. We must thank our guest for his assistance," said Hassan as he leaned back and placed a piece of duct tape over Eian's mouth. "We will be back to collect you two in an hour or so."

In a matter of minutes, they exited the car and climbed a small hill overlooking Shannon's farm.

It was time.

CHAPTER 26

Present Day - One km west of Castletownbere, Ireland

Jim had driven no more than 100 meters before the car suddenly sputtered to a halt right in the middle of the road. He eyed the gas gauge but it still showed half full. *Are you kidding me*, he said aloud before he banged his hands down on the steering wheel in frustration. He had to hurry. Nora and Eian were most likely in danger. He reached under the dash and pulled the hood release and quickly exited the car. Not that he was a car mechanic by any means but at least it was worth a look. Something could have come loose. He raised the hood and eyeballed the engine but couldn't find anything out of place. He fiddled with a couple of wire bundles resembling anyone who was totally inept at car mechanics. His *ah ha* moment came when he noticed daylight coming thru where his first bullet had entered the front quarter panel. Following its trajectory he noticed the bullet had entered the fuel pump. Jim stepped out from under the hood and looked behind the car and noticed a thick trail of gas from where he had driven.

The car was no longer an option. With no other traffic on the desolate stretch of road to bum a ride, he had no choice but to jog or walk back to town.

Either way, time was slipping by. He had to reach Nora and Eian before anyone tried to kill them.

CHAPTER 27

Present Day - MI-6 HQ: River House, London

Roscoe Hopkins knocked on the door of Sir Robert John office, him on the phone. Hopkins held up a Red Folder for his review. Sir John motioned him forward as he continued to speak. Hopkins was aware it was Benny Machaim of the Israeli Mossad on the other line.

Sir John held his hand over the mouthpiece of his phone. "Why do you find it necessary to burst in here while I am on the phone with a peer?" he said slightly agitated as he took the Red Folder offered by Hopkins.

Hopkins pointed to the folder. "I would read that, now, sir," he replied."

Sir John scanned the message before he looked up to Hopkins, nodding his thanks. He then turned his attention back to Benny Machaim. "Benny we seem to have a bit of a situation evolving here. One of my agents is down. It seems in the same area we were asking for your assistance a bit earlier. You said that you have several assets already in the area. Does you offer of assistance still stand?"

Sir John waited several seconds as Benny replied. 'Good, very good. I knew we could count on you."

CHAPTER 28

Present Day - MacCarthy's Pub and Grocery

Castletownbere, Ireland

Jim jogged to the outskirts of town, the 9mm securely tucked into his waistline. It had only taken him ten minutes to jog the distance from the Glebe Graveyard, where he left the snipers car with a bullet in its fuel pump. He now noticed a commotion at MacCarthy's near the town square. "That's where we left Eian earlier this afternoon," he said aloud with a look of worry on his face. He broke into a full sprint. Within a minute he was at the edge of a growing crowd outside the Pub as they watched the medical examiner wheel out a body with a white sheet spread over its length.

Someone in the crowd said there was two bodies, a man and a woman. Jims mind raced. His first thought was Nora and Eian. *But they only had a ten or fifteen minute start on him.*

As the medical examiner pushed his gurney containing the body up to the back of his station wagon the sheet slipped off to reveal the barmaid from the previous night.

A collective gasp was heard from the crowd. To Jim it was a sign of relief that it wasn't Nora.

Jim eased his way through the crowd and approached the town's sole Garda, or Irish police. "Excuse me, officer," he said.

The policeman ignored him for the moment as he eyed his towns first two murder victims in over 20 years. He personally knew both of the victims as he frequented the Pub most nights, as did most of the town at one time or another. He, along with most of the town, couldn't believe that three men would just burst into the pub and kill two of their friends and from what witness' stated, they took two hostages. He suddenly noticed Jim standing on the fringe of the crowd trying to gain his attention. It was at that moment he noticed Jim had a weapon in his waistband.

As the towns sole Garda officer he was authorized to keep a handgun in a lockbox in the station house. Actually not a station house but a rented room in the basement of the town's sole hotel. The town wasn't big enough for its own station house. But nevertheless, he never had cause to open his weapons lock box until today and this only due to the murders. He never thought the day would come when he had to carry a handgun. He pulled the 38 Smith and Wesson from its never used, shiny leather holster and pointed it at Jim. "Stop or I will shoot," he demanded as he hands trembled.

Jim watched as the crowd around him suddenly pushed back. Then he realized he still had the 9mm in his waistband. "Okay, we have a bit of a misunderstanding here," he said as he tried to calm the Garda officer.

"I want you to kneel on the ground with your hands interlocked behind your head," the Garda officer demanded, his voice cracking.

Jim realized the officer was a bit nervous and didn't want to take any chances. He followed Garda officers command.

The officer kept his weapon pointed at Jim as he walked to the rear of where Jim knelt, reaching around his to his waist to remove his weapon. "Now why would you need to be carrying this?" he asked Jim as he held the weapon in front of Jims face.

"It's a long story," he began, but it's not mine.

The officer looked around at the crowd that had reassembled. "It's not his, he says."

The crowd laughed in unison.

"And we just happen to have two dead bodies from gunshot wounds and you show up with a weapon."

"I was outside of town at the Glebe Graveyard for the past hour or so," Jim replied. "I wasn't here. You have to believe me."

"Well for the moment you're coming with me to the station until I can get some help down here from Cork."

"But my wife and friend may have been in the bar when this happened. I need to make sure they are safe."

The officer handcuffed Jim. "You're going to the station until we can straighten this mess out. Were you aware that just for carrying an unlicensed firearm in Ireland means mandatory jail time? This isn't America."

A middle-aged women stepped forward after the officer had helped Jim to his feet, his hands secured with plastic riot control handcuffs. "Officer I saw everything that transpired at the bar and this man is not one of the suspects I saw fleeing," she said as she looked to Jim. Moreover, I saw him in the pub last night with his wife and their friend. He was buying shots for old man Lynch. He looks nothing like the men you are looking for."

Jim smiled as he nodded his thanks to the woman.

The officer steered Jim in the direction of the police station. "If you follow me maim I will take your statement. But he still has an unlicensed firearm charge to deal with."

CHAPTER 29

Present Day - Sheep's Hollow Farm, Castletownbere, Ireland

With its fertile soils, a temperate climate, and abundant rains, Ireland's southwest coast possessed the enviable natural advantages for farming or raising animals such as sheep or cattle. Aided by the moderating influence of the Gulf Stream, most crops grew easily in its climate. That is, after you cleared the abundance of stone that that seemed to always be more plentiful than the crops. Luckily, most of the farmers worked together on clearing acres of rocky fields, much like the Amish for a barn raising, dividing the land with dry stonewalls built from the rocks cleared from the fields. No mortar holding the stone together, just made by carefully selecting stones that balanced and 'sat' into the wall as it is built.

A slender woman in her late twenties was busy rebuilding just such a wall. She adjusted her Irish Wool Flat cap on her head so it covered her eyes from the rays of the morning sun, in the process pushing back her jet-black main of hair off her ivory-skinned face. Shannon Flaherty was considered attractive to most, if a bit hardened, dressed conservatively in a loose fitting work shirt, heavy gloves, and wearing her wellies due to the previous night's rainstorm. She found herself continuously repairing her farms walls due to them being unstable – a task that many farmers in the area had to undertake regularly if they wanted their animals to stay penned.

One of the walls 5-kilo stones slipped from her hands and fell into a puddle at her feet, splashing up muddy water onto her face. "Are you kidding me," she yelled in a soft Irish brogue to no one. Her only employee and the only one she could afford, an older gentlemen in his late 60's, had off on weekends.

She was working the lands her mother had handed down to her upon her recent death due to a hard fought battle with cancer. Her mother had inherited the lands from her mother before her, and hers before that. Some of the farms that permeated the area were handed down through at least 20 generations. Shannon's family could only trace theirs back 11 generations before losing track somewhere around 1710.

Shannon picked up the large stone that had dropped into the muddy puddle and placed it back in its rightful spot. She stood up and brushed the muck off her pants. She looked around at her 80 acres wondering what she was doing here. She had a business degree from Trinity University. She even had a life, one with a well-paying job in Dublin until her mother called her home to help with the farm due to her illness. Now she found herself working from sunrise to sunset. The chores seemed endless: feeding, shearing wool, giving medication, maintaining the farm buildings and stonewalls, and the one she loved least of all, managing the waste. She had had many offers to buy the property but she couldn't find herself parting with something that had been in the family for so many generations.

The sun was just setting as Shannon and her sheepdog Tom-Tom moved the sheep into their stone pens for the night. Upon closing the steel gate and latching it shut she started back to the farms two bedroom stone cottage she called home. She would make herself a quick dinner followed by a hot shower, to rid herself of the farm grime that seemed to infiltrate her skin, and call it a night. "Whoopi!" she said to herself as she walked down the dirt path leading to the back gate. *If I were in Dublin right now I would just be heading out for the night.*

****

FROM A HILLTOP overlooking Shannon's farm, Hassan, Kagen Sims, and Berk Logan eyed Shannon as she moved about her duties, watching as she and her sheepdog herded the sheep into their pens. "She looks to be done for the day, boss," said Sims.

"We can take her when she goes into the house," followed Logan.

Hassan nodded. He pointed to Logan "I want you to cut the phone line. Sims, I want you to take the silencer and kill the dog so the damn thing doesn't bark and warn her of our presence. Then, we all converge on the front door."

****

SHANNON HAD JUST cleaned up her dishes from an early dinner when she thought she heard Tom-Tom, her sheepdog, let out a yelp. "Poachers or a wild dog," she immediately thought. "Wouldn't be the first time." She grabbed her shotgun off the wall rack, expertly loading two shells in its barrels and placed two more in her pocket just in case. She opened the front door and stepped out into the early evening.

Hassan and Sims were not in place yet, they were just making their way to the house when the front door suddenly opened, the houses interior lights castings its glow down the driveway. They each dove behind some bushes that lined Shannon's car park. Hassan signaled to Sims that they were to take her alive. No shooting. Sims nodded in response.

****

SHANNON THOUGHT SHE saw something moving in the shadows of the night. She looked right and left. Somethings not right she said to herself. Tom–Tom should be making a racquet by now. She called out to him. "Tom-Tom," but got no response. She moved the flashlights beam down the drive only to see Tom-Toms' body laying limp. She cocked the shotgun. "Bastards," she mumbled under her breath. She had plenty of experience handling a shotgun. Mostly vermin. Shannon reached in the doorway for the phone. Luckily it was just inside the door. She picked up the receiver only to find the line dead. "That's strange," she said. 'That's never happened before. The electricity yes, but not the phone." Shannon grabbed her car keys. If her dog was dead and the phone on the blink, something was not right and she was not hanging around to find out. Her car was only parked 20 meters away by a small tool shed. Slowly she stepped out of the doorway and onto her gravel drive as she walked towards her Mitsubishi SUV. The gravel made a crunching sound as she walked. Above her in the nighttime sky, a brilliant half-moon provided just enough light to see the outlines around her property. She looked cautiously from side to side, not wanting anyone to surprise her.

****

HASSAN COULD HEAR Shannon as she walked closer, the gravel giving away her position each time she put a foot down. Using hand signals, he instructed Sims to distract her while he jumped her from behind. Sims nodded in understanding. Hassan held up five fingers as he counted down to zero.

****

SHANNON'S HEART raced as she walked towards her car. With the shotgun in one hand she removed the car bob from her pocket, using it to signal and unlock the car's front door. The vehicles lights also came on in response. Shannon unexpectedly heard a noise to her right; she could see an image rushing towards her. "Stop or I'll shoot," she yelled in a high-pitched voice. The image kept charging her. Shannon dropped the car bob and placed the shotgun against her shoulder. "I said stop," she yelled once more before she pulled its trigger, a loud blast was its response. It was the last thing she remembered as something metallic hit her on the back of the head, knocking her unconscious.

****

HASSAN LOOKED AT Sims as he lay dead in the driveway. "Idiot, I said to distract her not charge her," he said to the now dead body just as Logan ran up the driveway.

"What the hell happened?" Logan said angrily to Hassan as he tried to catch his breath.

"Your stupid friend charged the target instead of distracting her like I clearly stated to him." Hassan removed the 9mm from Sims clutched fingers, before he handed it to Logan. "It's yours now."

Logan fingered the 9mm with the silencer still attached as he looked to Hassan then Sims.

Hassan observed Logan, who was standing there looking as if he wanted revenge for his friend's death. "If you are thinking of using that weapon," he said as he pointed to the 9mm. "I'd have second thoughts if I were you. You know who my friends are. You wouldn't live a week until they found you."

Logan looked down at the weapon still deep in thought. This was not the time nor the place to extract revenge as he unscrewed the bulbous silencer, placing it in his pocket, and the 9mm in the small of his back.

Hassan nodded to him. "Wise move. Now go get the car so we can get our little hostage out of here."

Logan turned and hurried back over the ground they had covered earlier to where they had hidden the car amongst the hedges. In a matter of minutes he reached the car. "Hello my little birds," he said to Nora and Eian, who were still duct taped in the back seat. Logan quickly started the car, drove back to the dirt road, and then around the hill to Shannon's driveway.

****

HASSAN HAD WALKED back into the farms cottage looking for something to tie Shannon's hands and feet with. He spotted some thick hemp rope in the mudroom. *This will do nicely,* he said to himself. He then noticed the box of shotgun shells on the kitchen counter. He grabbed them as he formulated a new plan to disguise Sim's death. As he exited the cottage, Logan was maneuvering their rental car up the drive.

Logan stopped the car short of hitting the body of the dog that lay in his way. He quickly exited the vehicle and dragged the dog's body to one side of the road. Satisfied, he continued up to where Sims' body laid and where Shannon lay unconscious.

Hassan made quick work of tying up Shannon's feet and wrists before they carried her to the car, her body still limp. "You have some company," said Logan to Eian and Nora as they placed Shannon beside them in the back seat.

Hassan knew they had to hurry. It was a small community of tightly knit families. With Shannon having used the shotgun, he knew the sound of the blast reverberated through the hills. It was only a matter of time before a nosey neighbor tried to call or showed up uninvited.

Shannon woke up as they placed her beside Eian in the car. "What the hell happened?" she said, still feeling the effects of the blow to her head. She looked to Hassan and then to Eian seated beside her, him bound at the feet and wrists.

"Welcome, miss," replied Logan. "Say hello to your new partners," as he pointed to Eian and Nora. He then placed duct tape over her mouth."

Hassan pointed to the driver's side of the car. "Get in the car and let's get out of here."

Logan pointed down to Sims body. "What about him," he replied angrily. "We can't just leave him lying there."

Hassan eyed Logan. "You are right," he said in agreement as he looked around the yard. "Drag his body over to the tool shed while I turn the car around."

Logan did as he was instructed. Satisfied, he made his way back to the car.

Hassan pulled the shotgun from the seat beside him, placing two new shells inside its barrels. He then handed the weapon to Logan. "Shoot this into the ground," he said.

Logan had a puzzled look upon his face.

Hassan's eye narrowed. "Simply point the gun towards the ground and shoot it."

"You're the boss." A loud blast reverberated through the hills as Logan followed Hassan's instructions.

Hassan withdrew the 9 mm from the base of his back and took aim at Logan. "Sorry, my friend," he said as he placed two well-aimed shoots into Logan's head.

Hassan wiped the gun handle clean of his prints. He then exited the car and walked over to where Logan had dragged Sims' body. He placed the weapon in Sims' dead hand before he held it up and fired off one shot to get some residue on Sims' fingers. Hassan dropped the pistol beside Sims' body. Now it would look as if the two men had a lover's quarrel with the two of them shot each other in the process.

Hassan smiled at his brilliance. He got back into his car and drove down the driveway. He had to make it to his safe house before anyone found the bodies at the farm.

He had three new victims in the backseat.

Now it was Jim Dieter's turn.

CHAPTER 30

September 1944

13 km south of Munich, Germany

Over the course of two long weeks, using a combination of his Vatican diplomatic immunity, cartons of cigarettes, bottles of Whiskey, and precious diamonds, Perluci was able to cajole his way through various German Army roadblocks and reach just over the halfway mark to his destination. He avoided the main autobahns as he maneuvered to the west of Warsaw, then onto Prague, Dresden, and Munich. And for a price, he was able to locate black market petrol at towns just outside of army posts. Of course, he overpaid the already exorbitant rates so no one would ask any questions. Perluci also had a list of churches closed in the late 1930's by Hitler's vengeance against religion. Monasteries and convents were targeted for expropriation. With this in hand, he was able to seek shelter in one of the many boarded up structures. For most of his stays he choose to arrive at dusk. Nobody would ask questions with a German Army truck parked on its premises. Perluci just desired a roof with four walls and if lucky, a small wood burning stove. Nothing much.

He was pleased with himself as he drove a desolate road just south of Munich, the day starting to turn to night. Not once did he have to use lethal force and hurt anyone. *From your mouth to Gods ears*, he said to himself as a roving SS patrol roadblock suddenly appeared just ahead of him. Their motorcycles were positioned so they blocked the road. The SS were the ones Perluci feared the most due to their fanaticism. At this late stage of the war, with their side losing, they liked to administer *on the spot justice*. They had no desire to take prisoners. Perluci hastily slipped his Beretta out of its shoulder holster, laying it between his legs and out of site but providing easy access if needed. In the past 30 minutes he had passed only one other vehicle. Which seemed about right with a genuine lack of petrol in the country. However, it also meant he was isolated. Just the SS troops and himself; not an ideal situation. He slowed his vehicle as the lead soldier held up a small *Halt* sign with one hand and his other out straight a clear indication for him to stop. Perluci could see at least two additional soldiers in the patrol as he slowed to a halt. One soldier now stood in the front of his truck, his machine pistol unslung and the other two each positioned themselves at the passenger and driver's side door.

The sergeant in charge stepped up and onto the trucks running board. He unslung his weapon to appear more menacing before speaking. Papers, please," he said curtly.

Perluci smiled as he handed him his Passport. "Sergeant, you will notice that I have diplomatic immunity."

"This is wartime, Father," he said looking at Perluci in his disguise as a priest then his passport, then back to him. "We have many people with diplomatic immunity and a rampant problem with thieves driving these back roads." Both of the other soldiers laughed aloud. "We happen to be the latter ones."

Perluci realized what they sought. With the war nearing an end, they required anything of value to trade. "In the back I have a crate of whiskey. Good American whiskey." He lied. But they took the bait anyway.

"Out of the truck," the sergeant demanded, as he stepped down. They wanted to see what other riches he had in the back of his truck. Perluci had no choice but to allow them access.

With the sergeant's movement, he provided Perluci with just enough time to place his pistol back under his black suitcoat and into its holster. "Yes, of course," he said as he exited the truck. Perluci scanned the woods to see if any additional soldiers lay in wait. Satisfied, he led them to the rear of the truck, quickly untying the canvas cover and pushing it aside.

"Which crate has the whiskey?" demanded the sergeant.

Perluci pointed to the crate nearest them. "I'm not in as good a shape as yourself. Maybe you or your men could lift it down.

One of the other guards roughly pushed Perluci aside. "I will get it, sergeant," he said as he jumped up and into the truck.

The second guard unslung his weapon to help the first.

The sergeant turned back to face Perluci. "What's in the rest of the crates? He demanded.

Perluci smiled at him. "Just clerical files, religious items of importance" he said. "I am the one who had responsibility to evacuate our Consulate in Prussia before the Russians took over."

It was the sergeant's turn to smile, as he still faced Perluci. "Open the rest of the crates after you find the Whiskey," he demanded of the soldier in the truck. "I don't trust this little shit."

The soldier in the truck couldn't find any tools to open the whiskey crate. "Sergeant, there is nothing back here to open the crates with."

The second soldier jumped up and into the truck to help search for tools.

Perluci saw his opening and moved in like a shark. He turned to the sergeant, and then pointed to where the spare tire was bolted to the undercarriage of the truck: "If you look under the tire you will find a tool box."

The Sergeant now unslung his machine pistol. He walked over to the trucks undercarriage and looked under at the spare tire. "I don't see any tool box in here," he said before turning back to face Perluci.

Perluci was quick to the draw as he withdrew his pistol, shooting the sergeant with a single shot to the head, then without hesitation the other two soldiers in the back of the truck before they could react.

"Never turn your back on someone like me," he spat out at the sergeant's dead body. He climbed up into the back of the truck and pushed both soldiers' bodies out and onto the road.

Perluci then drug the bodies one-by-one to the side of the road before he pushed them down a steep embankment. No one would find the bodies. He was sure of it. Next he pushed their motorcycles off the road and down the same embankment. Satisfied with his work, he climbed back into his truck and drove on.

Over the course of the next few days, he would be forced to drive through the Brenner Pass. There was no way around the Pass. No back roads. The SS would have much larger roadblocks and more frequent stops. It was one of the only connections between Austria and Northern Italy that didn't involve railroad tracks or a tunnel.

Only then could he get his precious cargo south to Italy.

CHAPTER 31

Present Day - Castletownbere, Ireland

Jim sat handcuffed to the police officers desk in his *station house*, a room the size of an average kitchen. He was getting visibly frustrated as it approached his fourth hour of looking at the same two metal desks and a holding cell that would have looked more at home in 1880's Wyoming with its padlocked iron bar door. That and the fact that the cell could fit maybe two prisoners if the police officer stopped using the cell for storage of boxes upon boxes of official paper records.

The story of how he had acquired the 9mm was now long finished. Also, the woman who witnessed the actual crime had come by to vouch for Jim. It also helped that the woman was a 2nd cousin of the officer. Jim had hoped the officer would have released him on his own recognizance. But things tended to mover slower in Ireland; *a lot slower.*

The phone suddenly rang to life. Jim sat listening to the officer as he spoke on the phone. At first it seemed like a prank call with the officer not believing the identity of the person on the other end. However, after a few minutes, the officer sat at attention in his chair. After about five minutes, the officer hung up the phone. He was sweating profusely. He reached into his desk and pulled out a bottle of Jamison, along with two small glasses, pouring a small amount into each.

"It seems as though you have some very high up friends." He reached over and used his key to unlock the handcuffs around Jim wrists. "You are a free man, Mr. Dieter." He slid the glass of whiskey across to Jim. "That person on the phone was Sir Robert John, Head of MI-6. He said you are essentially working with his people *on* a *need to know business*."

"How do I get myself into these situations," said Jim to the police officer. He took the glass, "Slancha" he said, cheers, as they both consumed the glasses contents.

"Please accept my apologies," said the officer as he handed him back his wallet and cell phone. He paused for several seconds as he looked at the confiscated 9mm before following Sir Robert John's advice and returned the weapon to Jim.

Jim thanked the officer, realizing the tight situation he was in. Weapons are a no-no in Ireland. Sir Robert John must have really told him a whopper. When Jim turned on his iPhone he noticed he had five missed calls from Nora. He quickly called his voicemail only to be rewarded with Nora informing him that she, Eian, and Shannon were being held hostage by a lunatic. She provided the address where they were being held and she stressed that only he was to come. She also provided him with Hassan's cell phone number. Moreover, he couldn't tell a soul of their plight. No one else, or they would be dead.

Jim hurried outside before dialing Hassan's number.

After five rings, Hassan picked up. "Hello, Mr. James Dieter," he said as if they were old friends. "So nice of you to call."

Jim wanted to reach through the phone and grab Hassan's neck but he realized he was in a *tight situation*, at least that's how he would have phrased it in the old days when he was a US Navy SEAL. But never in all of his years did he have to face a situation where his wife was one of the hostages being held by a mad man. This was a first. "May I ask why you are holding my wife and friend?"

"Don't forget, Shannon Flaherty, the deceased Daniel Flaherty's daughter," Hassan replied. "I have all three of them."

Jim realized he had to keep his cool. Make the other guy think he is in charge while you steer the conversation. "Is this a negotiation? What will you accept from me to gain their release?" asked Jim, his voice steady.

"You, and you alone will meet me at my leased cottage. I am texting you the directions as we speak. I will give you one hour to get here or one of them dies."

"I have to rent a car. I have no wheels," said Jim, his voice rising. "I need more time."

Hassan paused on the other end. "All right, I will graciously provide you with two hours, no more." He then hung up.

Jim then did a U-turn back to the station house. "Can you tell me where I can get a rental car?" he asked the officer.

****

NO MATTER HOW many times he visited Ireland or England Jim always became confused at the roundabouts. After three roundabouts, two near misses, and a heated exchange of words with a burly truck driver Jim exited the asphalt main road onto a rutted dirt road. *What a changeover* he thought. How could this road even be on a map? According to his iPhone, he was only three kilometers to the agreed upon meeting place, a small coastal cottage. He mentally reviewed his options as he took in his environment. He started with good old number one: there were no options. The other party held all of the cards. Option two: he was screwed when the other party held all of the cards.

The sunken lanes, hedgerows and rock-lined properties, making his travel a pitifully slow affair.

He struggled to follow the phones directions as it constantly updated due to his remote location. He hoped he typed the address in correctly. When the kidnapper first called he was so infuriated and a bit overwhelmed that he might have typed in the address incorrectly.

Finally on his left hand side he noticed a sign announcing 'Becks Cottage'; he turned into its crushed stone drive. After 10 meters, Jim stopped the car, turned off his cars lights, and then the engine. Looking at his iPhone he still had 100 meters until he would reach the cottage at the top of the drive. From his location he couldn't view the house due to all of the overgrown shrubbery on the property. But that also meant they couldn't see him. He sat in the car for a brief moment as he gathered his wits about him. He had no idea how many bastards he was going to face. At least he had a knife he bought in a fishing shop and the 9mm from the dead MI-6 agent. But he had no intelligence. Didn't know the layout. And they had somebody he was emotionally attached too.

Jim started the car back up and continued down the drive until the cottage came into view. It was definitely in a secluded location; the cottage smack in the middle of scattered rolling hills and open fields. From what he could see, the cottage had seen better times. As he slowly drove by he noticed at least two lights were on. Jim drove to the stonewall fronting the cottage, parked the car and exited with the hope of scouting the area when the front porch light came on and the front door opened.

Nix that idea. They knew he had arrived. It was time.

Jim cautiously walked up the gravel path to the cottages wooden steps leading to its porch. He paused listening for any telltale sounds before he walked up the wooden steps, each step creaking in announcing his position. He once again paused at the front door as he suddenly remembered a story from Sunday school about the Roman Emperor's throwing Christians to the Lions. Obviously he was playing the part of the Christian.

He walked in.

Hassan stared at Jim from a chair he occupied in the living room by a blazing fireplace, on his lap rested a gun. On a sofa fronting the door sat Nora, her feet and hands bound at the wrist.

"Come in, James," said Hassan. "Or may I call you Jim?"

Jim stood in the living room doorway, his eyes were adjusting to the dim light of the room. "You can call me whatever you want," he spat out, "as long as you let everyone go."

Nora made eye contact with Jim and then she looked swiftly to her right.

Jim nodded slightly to her in acknowledgment, her indicating to him that there were others in the house.

"Okay, I will call you Jim," said Hassan as he acted the gracious host. "Please do sit down, Jim. We have much to discuss."

Jim stared hard at Hassan. "Just tell me what it's going to cost for my wife's, Eian's and Shannon's freedom," he said angrily. "You obviously want something from me."

"Nothing will be accomplished until you sit down and drop your rash American attitude." Hassan used his weapon to point to a leather chair situated across from him and Nora.

Jim could see he held no cards in the game. He sneered at Hassan and sat down as instructed. "Okay, enough with the silly games. What do you want?"

"Isn't that better? We can talk as two adults."

"Yeah, real nice," replied Jim sarcastically.

"You obviously want to know the reason why I have invited your wife and yourself to sit and have drinks with me," Hassan said. At that moment the kitchen door opened and a man brought out a glass of Guinness, he placed it on the table in front of Jim and then placed a glass of Jamison in front of Hassan. On Hassan's nod the man retreated back to the kitchen.

"My apologies, but your wife seems to be unable to enjoy a beverage with us. And Eian and Shannon are a bit tied up in the kitchen."

Jim looked at Nora, her eyes smiled back in response. He was going to rescue her no matter what it took.

Hassan followed Jim's gaze. "She is a beautiful woman, Jim. My only hope is that nothing will happen to her."

Jim had had enough as he jumped up out of his chair and in one swift motion pulled his knife from his pocket and charged Hassan. This was anticipated by Hassan as one of his men suddenly popped out of a closet, his Uzi burping a single burst over the head of Nora.

The burst caught Jim by surprise as he pulled Hassan up from his chair, strangely he offered no resistance, Hassan now with a knife to his neck. "Tell your man to back off."

"I will do no such thing," he replied.

Another man eased the kitchen door open with two barrels of a shotgun aimed at where Jim stood.

Hassan pointed to his men. "You seem to be outnumbered and outgunned. Due to the amount of funding I am providing, the IRA has lent me a few of their men."

Jim looked at Nora, hers eyes wide. "Free Nora, Eian, and Shannon, and I free you," he said, as he pressed the knife into Hassan's neck just enough to allow a trickle of blood to flow. "It's a simple trade."

"Jim, I am prepared to die," Hassan replied. "The question is are you and your beautiful wife?"

"I'd listen to him if I were you, friend," said one of the IRA men. "We have already been paid for our portion of the job. So if you kill Hassan, I kill you and your lovely little wife. Seems like such a waste."

Jim could see he was once again on the losing end and getting nowhere. He removed the knife from Hassan's neck and expertly threw it into the wooden floor where it stuck. He returned to his leather chair and flopped down. "Your move," he said to Hassan in disgust.

Hassan used his fingers to wipe the blood from his neck, smearing the blood on the fabric of the chair where he sat. He smirked at Jim as if he had a secret. "I anticipated your little show. That's why I had my man in the closet. I guess your wife using her eyes to point him out didn't register when you first came in."

Jim had noticed. But he had thought she was indicating the kitchen.

Hassan produced a big toothy grin. "Let us get down to business. You and your Israeli friends killed the Hezbollah chief in Lebanon several months ago. That was a brilliant piece of work on your part. A missile strike while he was holding a meeting of his senior commanders. Because of it, the new boss who took his place wants you dead. And that is the reason why I am here. I could simply shoot you now and be done with it. But I am a reasonable man. I think we can both profit from misfortune."

"Either kill me or get to the point, because you are really starting to piss me off," Jim spat out.

"I like you, Jim Dieter. You simply cut through all of the formalities. *The bullshit* as you Americans have a tendency to say. All right I have a proposition for you. You are to perform a simple job for me. Once the job is complete your wife, Eian, and Shannon will continue to live prosperous lives. If you choose not to perform the job, well, that would be unfortunate. I would be forced to kill all of you here and now."

Jim looked hard at Hassan, then his armed men. "How do you expect me to respond? You win. I will do what you say," he said. "But remember this, if our paths ever cross again after I perform this job, I will kill you."

"I would expect nothing less," said Hassan as he reached over and removed the tape from Nora's mouth. "I knew we could come to an arrangement. If I were in your position, I would respond in the same manner. You and I are not that different, my friend."

"Let's get one thing straight. I am not your friend," Jim replied. *"And we are different."*

"Just a manner of speech I assure you," Hassan said. He stood up and walked over behind where Nora sat. "Now for the job at hand. It is simple, really. You will go to the continent and rob a plane for me. Not just any plane, but one containing over $50 million in diamonds."

"Is that all?" Jim replied sarcastically.

"See, even you acknowledge it is a simple job. I will even assist you by providing a crew of four. All top shelf talent but in need of a leader such as yourself."

Jim studied Nora before he replied to Hassan. "I work alone. I don't require anyone else's cast offs."

"But I think you do, and per my orders, you will take them onboard." Hassan stood up and directed his man to take Nora to the kitchen. The second man kept his weapon trained on Jim. "You will see your wife and friends again when you complete your job." With that he dropped a folder with all of the details of the operation on Jim's lap.

"My I ask a simple question?" Jim asked.

"But of course, we are all good friends now, aren't we?"

Jim ignored Hassan's comment and pushed on. "Why are you fixated on me and those close to me? Why kidnap my wife, Dan's daughter, and Eian?"

"That's a reasonable question. And it deserves a reasonable response. You had great success in tracking down and retrieving Bormann's gold; and in the process had my boss, at the time, eliminated. So you basically stole something people said didn't exist. You also assisted the Israeli's in killing the top echelon of Hezbollah. From that

155

moment I knew you, when the time arose, were the one person who could help enrich my personal coffers. And most importantly, keep it all a secret."

"Your personal coffers? So you don't intend to share the monies from the diamond heist with anyone?"

"You are correct. My boss, the new Hezbollah chief, paid me a very generous sum to come here and eliminate you. But I am putting you to work for me."

"So you can take the diamonds and run?"

"Yes, and you and your little group of friends get to stay alive while I go live on my own private island somewhere. Everybody is happy."

"Except your boss. No doubt he will send a hit team to search for you."

"And he will never find me. So, are you going to do the job for me or do I kill you all now? Your choice."

"Like I said before, you hold all of the cards. So, I don't have a choice. I'll do it. But if I were you, I would grow eyes in the back of your head because I will always be coming after you."

Hassan nodded. "As should you. I can only wish you good luck on your inevitable success, Jim. You may leave now. Follow the guidance I have provided in that folder you hold. For now, I have transportation arranged to take you to Belgium. After that, I will be in touch."

Jim walked out the door with a sideways glance, not trusting the man with the Uzi. "Remember what I said, Hassan. You better always be looking behind you."

CHAPTER 32

October 1944 – Innsbruck, Austria

Perluci accomplished the drive from Munich to Innsbruck easy enough. Now for what lay ahead he would need assistance. *Special assistance.* There were many such groups, but most were in their infancy. He would follow one that the Vatican had agreed to assist. The ODESSA, from the German Organization der Ehemaligen SS-Angehörigen, meaning "Organization of Former SS Members," was the largest that stood out from the rest. It was also the best financed and most lethal. In early 1944, a full six months before Perluci stole his precious cargo, a group of SS officers realized the war was going to end badly for them and decided it best to start an international Nazi network for use after the war. The purpose of the ODESSA was purportedly to help coordinate secret escape routes to allow SS members to avoid capture and prosecution for war crimes. They would then escape to

Latin America or the Middle East, where governments were known to be receptive to their Nazi ideologies.

It's also when they first made contact with Vatican officials, Perluci being one of them, to seek out their assistance. They also approached many high-ranking politicians and law enforcement officials who were inclined to accept bribes to aid in their members escape.

ODESSA was ingenious in its methods. They began using German civilians who had been hired to drive German Army trucks on the autobahn between Salzburg, Innsbruck, Milan, and Genoa for delivery of *'Signal,'* the German Army propaganda magazine. Most of the drivers were ex-SS soldiers who were discharged due to wounds; ODESSA made sure of this. Now with their drivers in place, the trucks carrying 'Signal' magazine also was able to smuggle whatever the SS needed, whether it be human or pilfered riches; cargo that had to escape the Allies wrath.

With everything legally in-place, the cargo was ready to start its move through the pipeline, or as it was more commonly known as, *the ratline.*

It was agreed to by the ODESSA hierarchy that Antonio Perluci, of the Vatican Intelligence Bureau was to be one of the main points of contact for coordinating the escape routes. With Perluci's insistence, The Vatican had agreed to allow certain churches and monasteries to be used as waypoints along the primary routes of escape. Here any cargo or persons could move from location-to-location using the cover of darkness without drawing scrutiny. Each stop would be able to accommodate them anywhere from a single night up to several months. In addition, as long as a certain amount of monies were deposited in the Institute for

Religious Works (IOR) — commonly called the Vatican Bank, everything would be arranged from Innsbruck to Milan to Genoa. From there, they could choose to go to Paraguay, Lebanon, or Syria. Of course, Perluci, under the guise of a Vatican Diplomat, need not pay. He was the Vatican's point man on the whole project. His undertaking of the Amber Rooms movement was one of the first stress tests for the route.

And Perluci accomplished just that, using the Ratline to navigate through the most dangerous part of the route, the heavily guarded Brenner Pass in Northern Italy. Perluci exited near the town of Sterzing or as the Italians called it, Vipiteno.

It had taken Perluci an agonizing five days to navigate the short 20 miles through the Brenner Pass. With each day spent at a different Ratline associated church location where a barn was a necessity to park his truck and avoid the scrutiny of SS and Army patrols. Each night, under the cover of darkness, he drove to the next location which, due to security, was only provided by the church's pastor when he was departing. The pastor also provided him with a well-accomplished escort to help him navigate through the notorious backroads and cow paths he would drive to avoid any unwanted scrutiny. They would also phone ahead to inform the receiving pastor of *a delivery expected for that night.*

When he exited the Pass, he needed a rest after his long drive and wanted to implement phase two of his plan before he drove any further south. He easily navigated the streets of Vipiteno, a classic little village of medieval alpine architecture: crow-stepped gables, pastel colors and pretty wooden signs. At the end of the picturesque main street was a backdrop of snowy mountains, they turned off into a narrow alleyway and with his escort beside him they were able to locate *Our Lady of Marsh Catholic Church* easily enough. His guide jumped out of the truck, instructing Perluci to drive the truck to the rear of the church to its barn. This was Perluci's last stop on the Ratline. After this, it was a straight drive down the Autostrada, the Italian version of the German autobahn, to Vatican City.

Perluci drove to the barns doors, turning off his headlights as not to attract attention. By this time the parish priest and his escort were beside him, the priest fumbling with the keys before he finally opened the lock on the barn doors and swung them outward.

Perluci drove in. The priest shut the doors behind him.

The escort came up to the passenger side door, jumping up on the runner. "The priest says we are just in time for breakfast."

They hadn't eaten since leaving the last church eight hours ago. Perluci jumped down from the truck, walking around to his escort, them both proceeding out the barns side door, locking it behind them.

His escort led the way to the church's kitchen, evidently not his first visit. They could both smell fresh eggs and bacon cooking on the stove as they entered.

The long wooden kitchen table could seat at least 12 but was already set for only four.

The Parish priest rose from his seat to greet Perluci, before indicating for them to sit.

The rather large female cook nodded her head at them as she cooked.

"You are only the second person to use the escape line," the priest said. "I think we have worked out the so-called bugs."

Perluci grinned at him. "You have done well, Father Stefano," he said. "But I require something else of you." He looked to the cook.

"She can only speak Italian," said Father Stefano. "Have no fear in this church."

Perluci nodded. "I will need the services of at least two carpenters," he said. "They are people I will need to be, shall we say, *discreet.*"

Father Stefano looked to the escort then Perluci. "I have several parishioners who are presently out of work. So, this will not be a problem. Whatever you need, we will acquire for you."

"I will want them to start immediately. For my own purposes, I want ones that are not married. And I need to be on the road to the Vatican in two days so they must be able to start first thing in the morning."

Father Stefano rose from the dining room table, walking over where the telephone sat next to his book of parishioners. He quickly searched the book for a particular name. In less than a minute he located a name, dialing the number. "Rico, this is Father Stefano. I have a job for you and your brother. I need you here tomorrow morning at 7am. Bring your carpentry tools." Rico asked him several questions before Father Stefano responded. "Yes, yes. It's a job that pays very well."

Perluci interrupted Father Stefano. "Make sure they stop at a lumber yard and bring enough wood to build 20 medium sized crates."

Father Stefano relayed the information to Rico before he hung up the phone.

"You have your workers. Now let's eat."

CHAPTER 33

Present Day - Brussels Airport, Belgium

The Lektre Company was in the final stages of its yearlong contract to replace the airports perimeter fencing with the new Maxi-flex barrier, one that had a built-in intrusion detection system imbedded into its heavy gauge wire fencing and concrete barrier base. It was triumphed by its manufacturer as the latest in security protection. Unfortunately, the construction work also left numerous pieces of heavy-lift gear and Sealift storage trailers scattered along various sections of the fence, simply moving them as each section was replaced. For the Air Traffic Control Tower it presented them with a security issue as the equipment location blocked certain sections of the airports perimeter fence line from their direct view.

At the moment, the Air Traffic Control Tower had its hands-full with a halt to all incoming traffic until a Brink's armored van could load its cargo on Helvetic Airways Flight LX789, a Fokker 100 twin engine jet bound for Zurich. As part of its nighttime security procedures, the jet and its 52 passengers had already been pushed away from the airport's terminal by an aircraft tug prior to the armored vans arrival. Upon its arrival the armored van was directed into position by the ground crew as it backed up to the plane. Once in position, it took its guards 10 minutes to load $50M worth of diamonds onto the cargo hold. Once the armored van was clear of the aircraft, the pilot started his number one engine, followed several minutes later by his taxi instructions from the Brussels Air Traffic Control Tower.

Upon confirmation Helvetic Airways had started its taxi roll, the Air Traffic Control Tower allowed normal operations to proceed. They now turned their attention to the numerous aircraft presently in a holding pattern.

****

FROM HIS VANTAGE point near the fence construction site, Jim Dieter adjusted his L-3 night vision goggles to acquire a better view of the Helvetic Airways aircraft as it started its taxi to the main runway. He loathed having to use his SEAL Team training to lead a bunch of criminals but he had no choice. The team had been assigned to him by Hassan. They were nothing more than career criminals who were skilled in petty larcenies and auto theft. If he didn't follow through Hassan would kill his wife, Eian, and their former partner Dan Flaherty's daughter, Shannon.

Satisfied it was time, Jim used a small flashlight to signal back to his awaiting team. Using the latest in laser wire cutters, Jim effortlessly cut the fences one section while he awaited for his team to show. One hundred meters from where he stood, four masked gunmen observed his signal and quickly drove up in two black vehicles; a Mercedes Sprinter van and an Audi A6 car, each with the local police markings. Jim simply rolled the old fence back, creating a hole for the vehicles as they entered onto the airport property stopping only long enough for Jim to jump into the back of the Mercedes van. Once the door closed, both drivers turned on their blue flashing lights. They were only 1,500 meters from the main runway where Helvetic Airways now taxied in final preparation for take-off.

Jim had the one driver maneuver in front of the aircraft, forcing the pilot to jam on the aircrafts brakes in response. One of the Audi's passengers quickly exited the vehicle, her dressed as a policewoman, pointing to the number one engine with her right hand and at the same time using her left hand in a cutting motion to her neck, indicating for the pilot to shut down the engine. She then approached the pilots side of the aircraft and plugged in her communications set in order to speak with the pilot.

The pilot looked to his co-pilot, then back to the flashing blue lights of the police vehicle. "I guess we better shut down," he said as he shrugged his shoulders. The pilot then noticed the green light was blinking on his exterior communications link, which was normally used to speak with the ground crew, the link now established with the policewoman standing in front of the aircraft.

"Good evening," said the policewoman in near perfect English. "Your load was short two bags. We are here to load the remainder. It should only take five minutes and you will then be on your way."

"Understood," said the pilot in response, wondering why the tower had not informed him of the stoppage.

The Mercedes van quickly maneuvered to a position by the cargo hold located directly behind the number one engine. Jim jumped out of the van, running over to where he knew the aircrafts cargo hold release handle could be found. He pushed in the handle until it popped out. He then rotated it right, the hold door sprung open in response. He quickly maneuvered an extendable ten-foot ladder from the truck, creating a ramp from inside the truck up to the aircrafts cargo hold. From inside the truck two of the men scampered up the ramp and into the cargo hold. They quickly located what they sought, placing a small explosive on the safes lock. A small pop, and the safe opened in seconds. Inside, the safe there were seven, two-kilo bags of both industrial and high-quality diamonds. One guard took three bags, leaving the last four for his partner, before climbing back down the make shift ramp. In another minute, the ramp was placed back in to the truck and the aircraft cargo door closed and locked.

Up in the cockpit, the pilot's annunciator panel warning light stopped blinking signaling the cargo hold door was now closed and locked.

The *policewoman* outside the aircraft provided him with a thumbs up. "You are good to go," she said to the pilot. "Have a great flight." She then quickly jumped into the Audi and sped away, followed by the Mercedes van, each traversing the same route through the fence opening and quickly merging into the city's light traffic.

****

THE AIR TRAFFIC Control Tower had Helvetic Airways holding short of the runway as they allowed three of the backed up aircraft to land. The lead controller noticed the flashing blue lights near the front of the Helvetic Airways aircraft as the blue lights now departed. "What the hell is that," he said to his partner, now raising the aircraft on the radio. They watched as the blue lights sped through the fence line.

The robbery did not appear to disturb any of the passengers. In fact, the passengers were not even aware anything had transpired until they were informed they were returning to the terminal to disembark because the flight had suddenly been cancelled.

****

Brussels' police inspectors instantly suspected it was a professional job since no trace of the robbers was left behind. In a matter of hours they located two abandoned and torched vehicles in a suburban shopping center parking lot known for its frequent visits by the criminal element. The vehicles, a Mercedes van and Audi car both with official police markings, were believed to have been used in the robbery of Helvetic Airways Flight LX789.

****

ONLY A DAY AFTER the robbery, Jim Dieter sat lounging in the morning sun at an outside table at a Parisian Café. He was indulging in his morning expresso and reading the English version of the International Herald.

He smiled to himself as he read various articles about the Brussels Airport robbery, with most calling it a work of perfection.

Maybe I am in the wrong profession he thought as he folded up his newspaper and placed five Euros on the table. He had to make another phone call before he met with Hassan's crew of bandits.

Then he would show Hassan who was in charge.

CHAPTER 34

October 1944 - Vipiteno, Italy

The carpenters arrived promptly at 7am. Perluci smiled at their punctuality for punctuality was not something the local population was known for. As requested, their battered truck was loaded down with the required materials to build the crates.

Father Stefeno greeted Rico and his brother Nick warmly. He then introduced them to Perluci. "This is the gentleman you will be working for, Father Antonio Perluci."

Both brothers, upon seeing the white collar around Perluci's neck, removed their hats and bowed slightly, before shaking his hand.

Perluci smiled at both, his ruse of being a priest had come in handy once more. "Like Father Stefano said to you on the phone last night, I will pay you 30,000 lire (the equivalent of $300 US) for the job. No questions asked."

Both brothers looked at each other in shock at what would be considered two months wages before Rico spoke up. "For 30,000 lire," he said, "I would kill Mussolini."

Perluci knew he had found the right men for the job.

CHAPTER 35

Present Day - Brittany, France

Jim Dieter observed the two men and two women as they sat before him. Hassan couldn't have selected a scummier heist team, he thought to himself. The two men were former French Legionnaires whose checkered backgrounds were wiped clean, as promised by the French government, after their 8-year tour. The two women were petty criminals who could list grifter as their main source of revenue. Now they could add felony robbery to their rap sheets.

It had been a long four days since they had accomplished what the Brussels Times, Belgium's leading online English-language daily newspaper, had christened as "the heist of the century," stealing $50 million worth of both industrial and high quality diamonds. After the theft each had gone their own separate way, agreeing to meet in four days at the Hezbollah safe house in Brittany, a 10-acre estate in the middle of nowhere and the perfect location for the bandits to receive their cut of the robbery.

All they needed now was Hasan to show his ugly face. He had just texted Jim that he had taken the wrong turn off the main highway from Paris and would be 45 minutes late. And yes, he had Nora, Eian, and Shannon with him. He even sent a picture of the three in the back seat of his car, bound and gagged, a gun to their heads.

That's all Jim needed to see and hear. He just wanted them safe. He didn't care about himself.

He eyed the criminals before him as they lounged in the estates small, quaint, wine tasting room. More a small, 10 meter by 10 meter, stone home the owners had built on the edge of the property. A fire burned brightly in the room's stone fireplace. Each held a glass in one hand and a bottle of an expensive French wine in the other; Jim wanted both of their hands full. He had rehearsed this scenario over two dozen times. Each time with the same result. Now he was ready.

With Hassan being delayed, it only made his job a lot easier.

Jim clanged his crystal glass with a spoon to get their attention. "Ladies and Gentlemen," he said, looking to each, placing his glass back on the wooden bar in front of him. From underneath he pulled out seven, quart sized, clear bags of grade one diamonds, placing them on the bar so all could see their bounty from where they sat. "I want each of you to hold that baccarat crystal glass in your right hand, the bottle of Domaine de la Romanee Conti 1990, in the other." He paused for several seconds, the paused planned. "Now each of those bottles you are holding set me back a cool $20,000 apiece."

Each of his teammates seemed to eye the bottles more appreciatively now that they were aware of its cost.

Jim smiled coolly. After a couple of days, the mental rigors of his planning were starting to wear on him, making him feel like he had sandbags lashed to his limbs. The splurge on the expensive bottle of wine for each of his guests lifted a portion of the rigor. After all, it was Hassan's money, not his. It also allowed him to feel as though he had presented his guests with one last wish. Or were they Hassan's guests? Never matter.

Jim continued. "From what Hassan has told me each of you are the best at what you do. But as they say 'All good things must come to an end.'" He once again reached below the bar, this time pulling out an AK-47 he had secretly concealed earlier in the day. He walked out from behind the wooden bar, cradling the automatic weapon. Each of his teammates looked up in surprise, thinking at first it was a joke. Jim smiled at them as he leveled the weapon and callously proceeded to shoot each of them chest high, picking them off from right to left, in one long burst. The bottles and glasses they held in their hands crashed to the floor as each tried to reach for their own weapon. Not one of them was able to get off a shot before a bullet found them first. Satisfied with his work, Jim casually walked up to each body were they fell, removing a nine mm Beretta from his waistband, he placed a bullet in each as insurance.

"Sorry my little band of banditos but I have to answer to a higher boss," he said as he walked back to the wooden bar, placing both his AK and Beretta on its surface. He then looked to the source of greed that lay in front of him: $50 million in diamonds. Now he had it all. No split. Hassan had lied to his crew stating that each of the crew was supposed to be cut in for a cool $2 million each. As a matter of fact they were expecting their shares today. As per Hassan's instructions, they were to entrust Jim with the diamonds. And why wouldn't they listen to him? Hassan had assembled the team. He fronted the money for everything. He was their boss. Of course the diamonds were supposed to be allotted for the operations sponsor. Hassan had to be paid or else Jim's wife, Eian, and Dan's daughter would wind up like the rest of the team and be dead within 24 hours.

Unless Jim struck first. Now it was time to turn the tables on Hassan.

CHAPTER 36

Hassan was no fool of that he was sure. He trusted Jim no more than Jim trusted him. Jim looked down to his phone as yet another text came in from Hassan asking about his team at the estate and if they were ready to be paid?

Jim dialed the number Hassan had provided. Hassan picked up on the third ring.

"Have they been paid?" Hassan asked, recognizing the phone number as the one he had provided Jim.

"Yes, they have been paid in full," replied Jim smiling through his lie. "When will you arrive?"

There was a slight pause on the other end before Hassan replied: "If you think I am riding into an ambush, you are crazy," he said, laughing aloud into the phone. "The picture I sent of your wife, Eian, and Shannon were from my car in Ireland. I never had any intention of making an appearance in France"

Jim pulled the phone away in disgust. After several seconds he placed the phone back to his ear. "You double crossing, bastard," he said. "You promised me a trade of Nora, Eian, and Shannon if I performed the heist for you."

"What can I say, Jim," Hassan said. "I lied. You should have never trusted me. Now, what will you do with the dead bodies?"

"How did you know?" Jim said as he gazed about the room at Hassan's crew.

"I know your type," he said. "You would never let them live."

"So how are we going to do this exchange?"

"You will go to a private airport 10 kilometers from where you now stand. I will text you the address. There will be a private jet waiting to take you back to Ireland. When you arrive we will make the exchange: diamonds for your little flock. You should be here in about three hours."

Jim looked down at the weapons he had arranged on the bar top in front of him. The last time he had met with Hassan he lacked any real firepower. Obviously circumstances had changed. Hopefully in his favor. "I will see you in three hours," he responded confidently.

This time he would finish this once and for all.

CHAPTER 37

Present Day - Jerusalem

Benny Machaim pushed the papers in front of him away in disgust. He had had enough of desk duty and the mountains of paperwork that went along with it. *After five years as the chief you would think I could assign this to some lowly subordinate,* he thought as he shook his head. A slight knock at his door broke the anxiety for the moment, Benny looked up to see his executive officer, Moshe Eisen, as he entered the room. Benny pointed to the top of his desk. "Moshe, look at all of this. I thought the computer was supposed to make us paperless?" he said in jest. Moshe pointed to the wastepaper bin beside Benny's desk. Benny laughed aloud in reply. "I wish it was that easy my friend. One day you will find yourself sitting at this very desk and know what I am talking about." He indicated for Moshe to sit down. "I'm guessing from that mischievous grin on your face you have something of importance to share?"

Moshe nodded as he waved his paper notes in front of him. "You think I'm any different with paperwork?"

Benny laughed aloud. "You and I are part of the old-guard, my friend. He gestured to the outer office. "Some of the newcomers we have working for us have never seen the least bit of action. Still wet behind the ears. You and I are the only ones the Prime Minister would entrust with the details of job of this magnitude." He rapped his knuckles on the desk in front of him as if a courtroom judge ready for the proceedings to begin, and then stood up, walking over to look out his offices floor to ceiling window. "Okay, what did you hear from our contact?"

Moshe consulted his notes and started with the relevant points. "Of course you are aware of the Brussels Airport robbery?"

Benny had his back to Moshe as he continued to look out his window as he nodded once more, having read the full story in the Jerusalem Post only two days before. He raised his right hand and made a circular motion with his index finger as he indicated for Moshe to proceed.

"Well what you might not be aware of is this: after consulting with a few of our friends in the region, we have come to the conclusion that only someone with a Special Forces background and access to serious funding could have pulled off a sophisticated robbery like this."

"Any names pop up on the radar? I think Interpol might be of some assistance after we helped them nab the thieves involved with the Casino robbery in Monaco a few months ago."

"Well you'll love this. We think the whole operation was funded by the new Hezbollah chief, Sheik Naim Quasson." He looked up from his notes to see Benny now in deep thought as he stared out his office window at a grove of olive trees. "Boss?"

Benny turned to him with a smile on his face. "My apologies. I was just wondering how the new Hezbollah chief was able to pull-off a job of this magnitude after only a few days on the job? He would have had to contact the crew weeks ago to get this job rolling."

"So you think he went over his old boss' head?"

Benny nodded. "It's the only way. You would need specialized tools, trucks, airport diagrams and money to bribe officials. Then there is the surveillance, training, timing, crew schedules." He looked back out the window as if searching for something. "Think about it. To get all of this rolling and coordinated would take even our organization months to plan. So with that thought in hand, I think he may have had a hand in his predecessor's death. It's the only logical explanation. He was the real brains behind his passing."

Moshe placed his notes on top of his boss's desk. He nodded several times. "I can see your point. So then he can place the blame for his boss's death on Jim Dieter."

"And us. The State of Israel. The simple art of distraction, my friend. Just like a magician. I keep you looking in one direction and hide the real trick in the other. Now you are thinking like a true agent, Moshe. This Agency will be all yours one day but I'm not leaving until I'm confident you can take over. So, humor me. I want you to run with it. Let me hear your version."

Moshe smiled at his boss. This was the main reason he loved working for the man. He not only valued your opinion but also wanted to hear your thoughts. He quickly gathered his wits about him before he commenced. "A few months ago, Sheik Naim Quasson, was working on an intelligence job to ferret out those who may have infiltrated the Hezbollah. During the course of his inquiry he noticed several unusual links between his boss and one of our agency accounts. Links that upon further investigation involved certain bank transactions that enriched his boss' coffers many times over. So he caught his boss red-handed with his hands in the proverbial cookie jar. Being the power-hungry underling that he is, he sensed an opportunity to topple his boss. Now, how do you kill a national hero and not have any blame set upon yourself? This is where synchronicity sets in and suddenly an opportunity presents itself. Through his European network of sympathizers, Sheik Quasson heard rumblings about the opportunity to fund an airport robbery, this with the possibility of enriching his coffers many times over. He bites and wins. So now he is flush with cash, he can build-up his own network to help undermine his boss. He also handpicks Jim Dieter to take the fall; after all, he thinks Dieter was working with Israel. Our aborted raid on the Lebanese coast helped solidify that position."

Benny clapped his hands together, laughing aloud. "I can see the many years of you working by my side has rubbed off. Excellent! You and I are thinking in sync. So what would you do if you were in my position?"

"Is there something you're not telling me? Are you getting ready to retire?" queried Moshe with a hint of seriousness. "Seems like you are really testing your subordinate."

"Roll with me on this one, Moshe," replied Benny. "Our organization has a lot riding on how we handle this situation. I want to make sure you and I are on the same page."

"Sorry, boss. I was just joking." Moshe stood up and walked back over to the office window to gather his thoughts. "We have to expose the new Hezbollah chief, Sheik Naim Quasson, by informally letting our information about the diamond robbery slip out, and in the process help our old friend, James Dieter. Of course, not necessarily in that order."

Benny nodded. "I want you to personally run with this," he said as he walked over to Moshe and placed his hands on his shoulders in a fatherly gesture. "Because you are right, my friend. I am retiring. And if you perform as well as I expect, I will recommend you take my place as Director."

Moshe was taken back by Benny's sudden announcement. "You can't......"

Benny cut him off with a wave of his hand. "I'll get right to the point. I have cancer of the liver, my friend," he said, his ever present smile still in place even at a moment such as this. "My doctor said I have two or three months, tops. Those last months I intend to spend with my family. My grandchildren. Maybe do some traveling."

Moshe grabbed his friend in a bear hug. "You big son of a bitch." After several seconds went by, he pulled away, looking at his friend. "I will do as you say, boss. I think it best to activate Lieutenant Silverman's team and help our friend Jim Dieter."

"You will do fine, Moshe," replied Benny. "Now get out of here while I notify the Prime Minister of our intentions."

CHAPTER 38

Present Day - Castletownbere, Ireland

The pilot and co-pilot for the Gulfstream 550 obviously weren't employees of Hassan as they neglected to check Jim nor his bag for weapons before he boarded. Same thing at the arrival gate in Cork, Ireland, Hassan had a driver waiting for Jim. He too, neglected to check the obvious. This was just fine with Jim as they approached the cottage where Jim had left Hassan with Nora, Eian and Shannon only a few days ago. It made his job that much easier.

Jim had the driver of the car drop him off at the bottom of the long driveway leading to the cottage. With his bag in hand he started the walk up the 300 meter driveway. Jim tapped the back of his waist for reassurance, the 9mm still in its place. As he neared the cottage he reached into his bag and pulled out an AK-47 he had taken from the Hezbollah estate in France. He paused as he placed it behind a small bush thereby determining that this would be his likely fallback position. He then removed two V-40 mini-fragmentation grenades. Weighing just 5 ounces, they looked more like a modified golf ball. Jim placed one in each of his pants pockets. The only thing left in the bag were Hassan's diamonds. Jim removed two of the bags of diamonds, leaving the other bags behind, dropping them beside the AK-47. He was ready.

The driver had evidently called to say he dropped off his passenger as Jim noticed the front door ajar. He collected himself, took four deep breaths and walked in.

"Welcome, Jim," said Hassan as he rose from the same chair he had sat in a week ago. Jim raised one hand in the air, his other held the bag with the diamonds. Nora, Eian, and Shannon all sat on a sofa to the right of him, their hands and feet bound, duct tape over their mouths. Hassan walked over to where they sat and positioned himself behind the sofa, his gun pointed at Nora's head, his arm around her neck. "Jim, I think you will do what I say, when I say," he said, a smile spreading across his face. "I seem to have the upper hand."

"All right," Jim spat out, "I don't think I have a choice?"

Hassan lowered his gun using its barrel to point to several chairs in front of him. "Sit and be comfortable."

Jim looked to Nora, him smiling in reassurance.

She nodded in return.

"Now that you are comfortable," said Hassan, "I have a little story to tell you both."

Jim laughed aloud. "Why don't you just kill us instead of boring us with one of your stories," he said.

185

Hassan grinned at Jim as he moved over to Eian and in one single move brought the pistol down on Eian's head striking him on his left side. Blood slowly ebbed down his scalp onto his neck. "I have been told you are one tough, how do you say it in English? *A tough son-of-a-bitch.*" He laughed after he said it. "But not so much right now are you?

At that moment, Hassan's two IRA henchmen walk in with their weapons drawn. They take up positions that offered the best vantage points, right where Jim would have placed his men if the roles were reversed.

"Now my story begins," Hassan said. "Sheik Hassan Nasrallah, the one-time leader of Lebanon's Shiite movement, Hezbollah, was brutally assassinated. This attack has been blamed almost universally on Israel and the American sitting across from me, James Dieter."

Jim started to protest but Hassan fired a bullet at the feet of Nora.

Jim just glared at him. "You are repeating yourself, Hassan. We heard this all before."

Hassan continued. "We had a funeral for Sheik Hassan Nasrallah. A funeral we should have had, according to our religion, 24 hours after his death. But we had a hard time finding anything left of his body due to the airstrike the Israelis carried out. It took us a great deal of time to find anything that the labs could use to verify his DNA."

Jim smiled at the thought of them scraping the tissue of the Hezbollah leader from the rubble.

Hassan suddenly fired off another shot, this one at Shannon's feet. He then leaned down next to Nora's ear, his weapon pressed against her head. "Smile again and the next bullet enters your wife's skull."

Jim nodded. "I'll be a good boy and listen to your bedtime story."

Hassan continued. "The truth is this. My new boss, Sheik Naim Quasson, sent me here to kill you. Now the question is, do I follow through with his orders?"

Jim looked to Nora, Eian, then to Shannon. "May I speak?" he said, not wanting to jeopardize his wife's life.

"But of course," Hassan said trying his best to act the gracious host.

"I went and robbed the jet of its diamonds for you. Our agreement was that you would free Nora, Eian, and Shannon when I brought you the diamonds. Well here they are," he said before dropping the bag to the floor. "What else do I have to do?"

Hassan patted Nora on the head. "Good, that's the tame James Dieter I want to deal with. I don't want to kill anyone when we can all profit from our little adventure." Hassan moved behind Shannon. He used his weapon to pull her hair back. "Does this women even know you had her father, Dan Flaherty, killed on your last little adventure?"

Shannon's eyes bulged at him mentioning her father's name. She looked at Jim and then turned to look at Hassan.

"Yes, your father died six weeks ago because of that man across from you," he said as he pointed to Jim.

Shannon looked down to the floor, her eyes suddenly tearing up.

"She didn't even know about you and your little gang, did she? You are all strangers to her."

Hassan motioned for Jim to put his hands up as he walked out from behind the sofa and over to the bag Jim had dropped. He looked in at its contents. "Allow me to continue. I have recently heard from my sources that there were not $50 million but $100 million in diamonds on the jet that you robbed," he said. "But I only see two bags of diamonds, worth, I'd say, $20 - 30M." He picked up Jims bag and moved back behind the sofa. "If you want to save your beautiful new wife, and your two friends over here," Hassan said as he pointed to Shannon and Eian, "I would provide the other bags."

Jim looked over to Hassan. "Why not just kill me now?"

Hassan wrapped his arm loosely around Shannon's neck, his gun pointed to her temple, then he moved it slowly down to her neck. "Don't be a fool, Jim," he said in a lower tone.

"The rest of the diamonds for your three friends."

"And your boss, the sheik what's his name, is okay with you doing this?"

"Of course. You do the robbery, we keep the diamonds. With that kind of money, do you realize the kind of weapons we could buy for our fight against the Israeli's?"

"Weapons," Jim spat back. "Don't stand in front of your flag acting like a patriot. Your crooked sheik will use the money to line his own coffers or his Swiss bank account."

Hassan smiled. "No, he will only get half. He doesn't know about the $100 million in diamonds, he thinks the take was $50 million. I get to keep the other half."

Jim stared straight ahead. Avoiding eye contact with Hassan. "So you are going to steal $50 million from your boss? What about the two goons you have behind you for muscle? Now that they know your plan don't you think they will inform on you? Maybe even kill you and steal your diamonds?"

Hassan smiled as he suddenly wheeled around and shot both of his men, each with a single shot to the head, the force of the shots pushing both against the wall, their dead bodies sliding down to the floor at the same time. It all transpired in a matter of a second or two. Satisfied they were indeed dead, Hassan quickly turned to find Jim reaching behind his back.

"I wouldn't if I were you," he said, pointing his weapon at Jim.

Jim eyed Hassan. He was surprised how swiftly Hassan had turned on his own men. If only Jim could have reacted faster. But he never had a chance. He never saw someone react so quickly, like an old west gunfighter. "I guess now, the diamonds are all yours."

Hassan moved his weapon to the base of Nora's head. "Don't waste my time, Jim," he said. "There are consequences for every action. Get me the other $50 million in diamonds or your people will suffer the consequences of your actions."

Jim's eyes never left Hassan's. The man was a cold-blooded killer. But to kill your own men? Jim realized he had to act soon, or his friends would be next. "The rest are out front," he said looking as though he could kill Hassan with his bare hands if given the chance. "Let them go and you keep me as a hostage."

Hassan pulled the trigger once more; the shot missing Nora by mere inches.

Jim didn't flinch.

Nora closed her eyes.

"I have many bullets. We can play this game all day if you like."

Jim realized the man was a psycho. It wasn't the first time he came across someone comparable to him. He had to stall the only way he knew how. "All right, you win. I will lead you to the diamonds. They are just out front."

Hassan smiled once more. "All right, I am feeling generous. I want you to get up out of the chair, turn and face the door and then kneel. Very slowly now. No sudden moves."

Jim did as instructed. Hassan walked over removed the 9mm from the base of his back. "You won't need this now will you," he said before tossing it aside.

Hassan walked over and removed the tape from the mouths of Nora, Eian and Shannon. He pulled a small two inch knife from his pants pocket. He pressed the blade up to Nora's face. "It would be a shame to ruin such a beautiful face," he said as he allowed the blade to slice a line down her cheek, blood starting to flow. Nora let out a slight sigh in response. He then reached down and sliced the tie straps that bound each of their feet.

Jim led the way out the front door. Nora, Eian, and Shannon followed.

Jim's intent was to retrieve his stashed AK-47 before Hassan had a chance to respond. Then and only then would he even have the slightest chance to kill him without anyone else getting hurt. But he also saw how swift of a shot Hassan could be.

Jim led the way towards where he had hidden the bags of diamonds along with his weapon. Hassan pushed Nora, Eian, and Shannon ahead of himself.

Eian realized Jim needed a distraction. Just a couple of seconds worth. The telltale sign was Jim's slow deliberate walk.

When Hassan pushed Nora, and Shannon a second time urging them forward, Eian waited his turn. Hassan barked orders to each of them. "Spread out," he said. "Jim slow down. I want you just far enough ahead so I can kill you all if need be."

Hassan then pushed Eian but Eian overreacted and fell to the ground. Shannon and Nora quickly followed suit, diving for the ground.

Jim heard the commotion and dove for where he had hidden the diamonds and his AK-47, reaching the machine gun in time to bring it to bear on Hassan and let off a short burst.

Hassan dove for cover behind Nora, Jim's shots missing him but shattering the cottages front windows behind him.

Hassan grabbed Nora by the hair, him pulling her up. "Drop the weapon or she's next," he demanded, his weapon pointed at her ribcage.

Jim could see he was in a tough spot. He kept his weapon aimed at Hassan. "What assurances do I have you won't just kill us all and then take the diamonds?"

"I'm not playing around," Hassan said. "Drop the weapon or she's first."

Jim hesitated for a moment.

Hassan could see Jim still need convincing. He fired a round that pierced the floor only inches from where Eian lay.

"All right, all right," yelled Jim. He dropped the AK-47 to the ground in response.

"The diamonds, now, if you please," said Hassan haltingly.

Jim reached down and grabbed the remaining bags of diamonds that lay at his feet and tossed them one by one over to Hassan, each landing at the base of his feet.

Hassan smiled at Jim. "You see, I win every time. Now come out from the bushes and lay flat on your stomach like your friends here." Hassan could see the hesitation in Jim's eyes. He waited three seconds before he fired off two rounds only inches from Nora's head.

Jim followed Hassan's orders, dropping his weapon and walking over to where Eian lay, laying on the ground beside him.

"I hold all of the cards," said Hassan. "Now my boss wants you dead, James Dieter. I, on the other hand find a man with your skillset handy to have available. So when I return to see the Sheik, I will inform him that you were able to slip away into the night. And soon after so will I with my $50 million dollars' worth of diamonds." Hassan returned to the house to retrieve his bag, all the while keeping his gun pointed in the direction of Jim. He quickly returned to load the remaining bags of diamonds. In a matter of seconds he was in his car and driving down the driveway leaving behind a cloud of dust.

Jim sprung up and ran to where he dropped his AK-47. He grabbed the machine gun and returned to the driveway, firing off a quick burst at the car as it turned onto the road. He could hear the sound of glass shatter as he hit the rear window but the car kept going.

He turned his attention to his friends and his wife as they lay in the dirt on their stomachs. He pulled the duct tape from their mouths.

"He got away," Nora yelled. "You let him get away!"

"Wait a minute," Jim yelled in return. "He would have killed you if I didn't."

"That bastard," said Eian. "Jim's right, he would have killed us all. You saw what he did to his own people."

Shannon looked around at them all. "Who in the hell are you people and why did that man kidnap me, or us?"

Jim pulled out his pocketknife and cut the strap ties from around their wrists. After he was done, he said: "What do you say we all head back to Shannon's house and explain to this young lady exactly who we are?"

CHAPTER 39

Present Day - Tel Aviv, Mossad HQ

Moshe sat at gunmetal grey table in a windowless room reviewing reconnaissance photos with Lieutenant Benjamin Silverman. The ashtray on the table was filled with cigarette butts, the air about them was smoky. "I say we hit them at this point," said Silverman as he pointed to a crossroads.

"Our people say Jim Dieter killed the Sheik's assets at the Hezbollah safe house in France," Moshe said with a smile on his face. "And then torched the house."

Silverman looked at his boss. "I liked this guy from the first time I met him two months ago in Lebanon. We knocked back a few beers in the only Irish bar in the whole country. That's when I first shared with him Mossad's plan to aid him in acquiring the Bormann treasure. Not only did he obtain the treasure, he helped us take out the top tier leadership of the Hezbollah in the process. This is a person who is doing our work for us. We have to help this man and his family."

Moshe nodded. "I agree. Now, this is what you will do."

CHAPTER 40

October 1944 - Vipiteno, Italy

Perluci led the carpenters into the barn, its doors already opened by Father Stefano. As the carpenters walked in, a look of surprise spread over their faces when they saw the German Army truck.

Perluci stopped them. "I am paying you very handsomely for a one day job." He pointed to the truck. "Is this going to be a problem?"

Rico spoke for himself and his brother. "As I said earlier, Father. I would kill Mussolini for the kind of money you are paying."

Perluci nodded. He looked to Father Stefano. "Father," he said, "the three of us wish to be alone. We do not want to be disturbed."

Father Stefano smiled. "I understand completely, I bid you good day." With that, he turned and walked out the side door.

Perluci waved Rico and Nick over to the rear of the truck. He pulled back the canvas and then drew down the tailgate. "This is what you will be making," he said as he pointed to the contents of the truck. "The crates are all the same size so it shouldn't be too hard for you to build. Now lift the crate nearest the back and set it down were you can measure it. I will leave that one crate here with you while I take a drive with the rest."

The brothers lifted the wooded crate and placed it on the ground where they could easily measure it.

Perluci pointed to the crate and then the brothers. "You don't open the crate and nobody comes in here. And I mean nobody. Just the two of you." They both nodded to the simple request.

Perluci climbed up into the drivers cab and started the engine. "I should be back in less than five hours. Now open the barn doors and then close them behind me," he yelled above the whine of the diesel engine."

They once again followed orders, waiting until the truck had driven out before closing the doors.

Once outside Perlucci waved to his escort, him speaking with Father Stefano. "Let's go," he yelled to his escort as he pointed to the seat beside him. "We have a short ride to take."

The guide shook Father Stefano's hand as he bid him good-bye. As he entered the truck he looked to Perluci. "Where are we going? You have the carpenters working in the barn. I thought we still had until tomorrow?"

Perluci smiled at him. "You'll see."

CHAPTER 41

Present Day - Sheep's Hollow Farm,

Castletownbere, Ireland

Shannon, Eian, Nora and Jim sat around a worn kitchen table nursing cups of strong Irish tea. To the left of them a fireplace blazed away providing warmth on a chilly morning. Jim looked around at the houses *tired* interior thinking it had seen better days. Everything was shabby and in need of replacing. Especially the single pane windows, obviously the main reason for the roaring fireplace on an early fall day.

Jim had just finished explaining everything to Shannon. *Everything.* Even informing her about her father's involvement in the IRA. They were all stories her Mother had never relayed to her. Possibly for good reason. Upon Jim's conclusion, Shannon rose from her chair and walked around to where Jim sat. "Get up you big lug," she commanded. When he stood up she wrapped her arms around him. "I only hope when it's time for me to marry I meet a man as good as you," she said, tears welling up in her eyes.

Nora couldn't help herself as she rose from her seat and went over and wrapped her arms around the two of them.

Eian rolled his eyes wondering what the hell was going on. "Enough of this sappy talk and wipe away the tears, therapy session is over." he said.

Nora shot him a scowl that made him raise his arms in surrender. "I was just joking," he countered.

"Okay, okay, enough already," said Jim. He used the sleeve of his shirt to wipe away his own tears. "Shannon caught me at an emotional moment after the stories of her father, and our friend, Dan. I need both of you to sit so I can finish what we came over to Ireland for." He waited until they both sat down before he continued. "Now when we first came to Ireland I surely didn't think we were going to get shot at, kidnaped, shot at again, and have both the Vatican and the Hezbollah come after us. I guess when we throw a party, we really know how to throw a party. Only the best of the criminal element decide to show up."

"Yes, but it's not really a party because we are drinking this stinking tea," said Eian. "A nice beer would do me well about now."

Nora again shot him a scowl.

"Sometimes I don't know when to shut up," he replied in a barely audible voice. "My bad."

Jim removed an envelope from his jacket, holding it up for everyone to see before he handed it to Shannon. "This is the envelope that started our journey. Your father left this in a larger envelope addressed to myself. The three of us agreed that we would deliver the envelope to you personally. Well, you most of all know the circuitous route we had to take to get here. So young lady, here you are."

Shannon graciously accepted the envelope. "I don't know what to say," she replied with a smile as she placed it down in front of her. "You have all been so good to me. I feel as though it was entirely my fault for the muddle I got you into. Hell, I almost got you all killed."

A chorus of no's was their response. Nora reached for Shannon's hand for support.

"It wasn't your fault, Shannon," replied Jim. "I think it's the other way around; we almost got you killed."

Eian rapped his knuckles on the table. "You listen to me, young lady," he said in a stern tone. "Your father was a dear friend to us all. You are part of our little family. And we take care of our family."

A single tear flowed down Shannon's cheek. "I wish I could have known him like each of you. I just had the few stories my mom told me."

Jim used his index finger to tap the envelope he had provided Shannon. "Open something from the past. Open something from your father."

Shannon nodded in agreement as she eagerly ripped open the envelope. "I never thought I would hear from him again," she said, her eyes tearing up once more. "The last time I saw him I was a young girl and he and my mom were fighting. Something that seemed to happen with much frequency in those days." She looked inside the envelope and saw several sheets of paper. The first looked like a legal document that she placed aside; the second, a hand written letter she hastily focused in on. Tears were in her eyes as she quickly read the single spaced letter before turning it over to read the second page. After several minutes, she placed the letter down on the table. "My father said I was to trust you explicitly. So I shall. In his letter he said I was to take you to our back pasture where we would stare at the stars on a clear night. He said there is something out there that only I would notice."

"I guess we are going for a walk," said Jim.

Shannon led the way. It took them 10 minutes to negotiate the distance. When they arrived at their special spot, Shannon looked for something that would stand out. "Until I was six my father and I would stand here for hours looking up at the night sky. It was our little thing to do after dinner while mom cleaned up."

"Do you see anything out of the ordinary," asked Nora.

She scanned the stonewalls that lined her property before focusing in on one particular stone. One looked like it had writing on it. As she picked it up, she could see that it had her name etched on it. "It's got to be here," she said excitedly. "Look," she pointed to something sticking out of the ground where she had removed the stone. "It's a plastic bag with something inside."

She reached down and picked up the clear plastic bag. She looked at the bag, then to the rest of them. "It's like one of the Easter egg hunts he would set up for me."

She opened the bag and pulled out a single sheet of paper. She read it aloud so they all could hear. "If you are reading this it means I have truly departed from your life. So I had to pick the spot where we were both at our happiest. How I enjoyed spending nights out here with you under the stars. My only wish in life was to have seen you grow into the woman you are now. But enough. Onward and upward. You can tell that big lug standing next to you that the Amber Room is buried in the graveyard of the Reifenstein Castle church, just outside of Vipiteno, Italy. Grave markers 43 to 50."

"That son of a bitch," said Jim in a low voice. "He knew the whole time where Perluci buried the goods. He knew Perluci stole the Amber Room even before his untimely death."

Shannon continued. "And my little darling you are to inherit over two million in diamonds. Jim knows where to find them," she finished with a puzzled look on her face.

Nora and Jim looked at each other before Nora spoke first. "Now we know why he wanted the diamonds buried with him," she said in reference to when they buried Dan he wanted his cut buried with him.

"That sneaky son of a bitch knew this was going to happen all along," replied Jim. "The only way we were going to find the Amber Room was by bringing the letter to his daughter."

Shannon shook her head. "He wasn't serious was he?" she replied. "I mean not that I couldn't use the money. Just look at this place. It's a little run down."

Jim extended his hand. "We are going to take you to visit your father's grave. He is buried just outside of town. We have another surprise for you."

****

JIM PULLED ALONGSIDE of the road, parking near a soccer pitch. A sign on the right-hand side proudly proclaimed in Celtic: *Cill Achadh an Eanaigh*, or Glebe Graveyard.

Shannon was the first to speak. "My mom is buried here," she said. "She loved to walk the area. She said it brought her peace."

Nora and Jim looked at each other, exchanging a secret they alone shared.

Shannon led the way as they entered a small byway and walked the 200 meters to reach the cemetery. The pathway was little more than slightly trampled grass. A small wooden gate announced the entrance to the cemetery. The gate had an arch clad in overgrown ivy. As they pushed open the gate it was as if they were stepping back in time. The place was peaceful and overgrown in places with trailing ivy and winding creepers.

Jim now led the way just beyond the church ruins, over by the north-west wall of the cemetery.

"There he is," said Jim, pointing over to the grave so Shannon could see. They walked the 20 meters or so to the grave. The two shot glasses and a miniature bottle of

Jamison Irish Whisky were still resting against his tombstone.

Shannon hadn't visited her mom's grave in months due to the farm taking up most of her time. She started to cry upon seeing her mom's grave. "This is too much to bear," she began. "You aren't going to believe this but my mom's grave is right next to my dad's."

Dan looked at the stone, seeing Maureen O'Dywer. "I don't believe this," he said as he looked to Nora and Eian. "The only two graves to be dug in here for years and it was Dan and his wife."

Nora made a sign of the cross. "I just got the willies," she said. "We can't make this stuff up."

Shannon handed Jim the small spade he asked her to bring along from her farm. She walked over to her mom's grave touching her headstone and then her dad's. "Tell me we aren't here to rob a grave?"

"We only want something from its top layer," replied Jim. He leaned down and started digging in the middle of Dan's plot, right where he buried it six weeks ago. After several minutes, he hit something hard. He cleared the dirt away from around the edges of what he knew was a wooden box. He reached in and pulled out something resembling a children's shoebox. He brushed the residual dirt from its top before he handed it to her. "This is a gift from your father."

Shannon smiled as she took the box from Jim. "Thank-you," she said, "Thank-you all."

"Well go ahead and open it," said Nora.

Shannon obliged them by removing the lid from the top of the box. She reached in and pulled out a clear, sealed bag the size of a typical sandwich bag. "Oh my God," she said, her voice quivering. "These can't be real. It's some cruel joke on me."

Nora shook her head. "Trust me, dear," she said as she held up her own wedding ring, "They are all real."

"Should be close to two million US dollars' worth in there," said Eian.

Shannon had to steady herself by leaning on her dad's tombstone. "We are celebrating tonight. Everything's on me."

Eian grasped her by the arm. "Everything's on us tonight, miss," he said. "In honor of this man." He pointed down to Dan's grave. "Let's get out of here before those diamonds attract any unwanted attention."

Nora looked to Jim as Eian led Shannon out of the graveyard. "Attract attention?" she said aloud as she looked around at the empty graveyard.

"You heard the man," said Jim, laughing as he did. "Let's get out of here and head to town to celebrate."

Nora nudged Jim and waited until Shannon and Eian were out of earshot. "Dan knew the location of the Amber Room. There is only one reason why he played this little game of reuniting his daughter with us. He wants us to go find the Amber Room and return it to its rightful owners."

"Don't you think I know that?" replied Jim, a smile gracing his face. "I get to confront one of Dan's and Perluci's old arch enemies."

Nora had a skeptical look upon her face.

"The Head of the Vatican Secret Archives," he said the smile never leaving his face. "*Monsignor Canti La Russo.*"

Nora nodded as she started to understand Jim's train of thought. "You devious little man. You are going to make the Vatican think the Amber Room is still secure to throw them off the scent?"

Jim smiled at his wife. "It's time to extract some revenge for Dan and Perluci.

"And one Monsignor Canti La Russo is our target."

CHAPTER 42

Present Day - Vatican City

Jim paced the plush red carpet in the outer office of Head of Vatican Secret Archives, Monsignor Canti La Russo. He had been calling and leaving messages for two days hoping to speak with the Monsignor but to no avail. So he just decided on the spur of the moment to just show up, unannounced.

Jim discerned that only Monsignor La Russo, The Pope, and maybe 10 others were even aware of what lay locked up in the rear of the Vatican Secret Archives, in an area called the Red Badge room. Each incoming Pope was provided a brief tour of the Red Badge room. The room contained, according to his own source, the Amber Room panels amongst many other treasures. Of course his source, Perluci, was killed several months ago.

A women's hearty laugh from inside the Monsignor's office stopped Jim from his pacing. He decided to sit down in a worn leather chair just outside the office door. He could hear a muffled conversation followed by another laugh and then the door suddenly opened; out stepped a nun in the old-fashioned, head-to-toe, blue habit; Monsignor Canti La Russo was dressed in his formal long black cassock, a red rope around his waist signified his rank in the church hierarchy. He bid her good-bye.

The Monsignor then eyed Jim suspiciously. "Can I assist you?" he said politely. "Do we have an appointment?"

"Well yes and no, Monsignor," Jim said. "Yes you can help me but no I don't have an appointment. My name is James Dieter."

"You," said the Monsignor in a callous tone his politeness now gone. "I thought you had given up." Of course he was referring to the numerous messages Jim had left.

Jim smiled. "Just five minutes of your time, Your Excellency," he replied.

"Will you leave this office alone once and for all if I grant you the five minutes?"

"Most certainly, Your Excellency," Jim said with mock sincerely. He would bother the Monsignor as many times as he deemed necessary.

"All right then. Come in if you must," he said begrudgingly, holding the door open for Jim. "Please take a seat," pointing over to one of the rooms two leather chairs in front of his desk.

Jim was impressed by the man's office. Obviously, he held a high rank in the church's hierarchy. He briefly looked around, noting the hand carved desk, numerous pictures with various dignitaries on the walls, and a large picture window that looked out over St. Peter' s Square. Rank definitely had its privileges.

"May I first ask how you eluded the guards and the administrative staff downstairs?" the Monsignor inquired.

"I lied my way past," was his truthful reply. "I signed up for the private tour, told the guide I had to use the men's room when we were walking past the administration building, which happens to be where your office is located, and took it from there."

The Monsignor smiled at its simplicity. "From the ten messages you left me I would say the reason for all of the cloak and dagger is due to the Amber Room, isn't it?" he said, avoiding eye contact with Jim as he pushed some papers absently about his desk. "Just give it up, man! It was destroyed almost eighty years ago in an Allied bombing raid. Contrary to what you may have heard we simply do not have it."

Jim started to unbutton his shirt.

The Monsignor looked at him as though he were mad.

"My apologies," Jim said as he pulled files from where he had hidden them pressed up against his chest. He then dropped them on the Monsignors desk. "I tend to think differently, Monsignor. Since I only have five minutes of your time, may I start?"

The Monsignor looked as though he wanted to laugh aloud but thought differently. "By all means, please do."

Jim nodded. "As I see it, everyone who has been associated with the Amber Room or who had intimate knowledge of its travels since it first left Russia during the war has simply disappeared or died a very violent death."

The Monsignor folded his hands together as if in prayer or meditation, looking to the pure white ceiling of his office before speaking. "Since we have no knowledge of what you are talking about I will assume you are correct in your research."

Jim smiled as he continued, "Let's start with the man in charge of its safekeeping after it arrived in Königsberg in a highly-guarded German military convoy of looted art from Leningrad in the old Soviet Union, Dr. Alfred Rohde. In the convoy of trucks was the Amber Room panels. Dr. Rohde, as the director of the Königsberg museum under the Nazi regime quickly assumed control of the Amber Room panels; after all he was one of the world's foremost authorities in Amber art. The Russians also were aware of this and at the wars conclusion both Dr. Rohde and his wife were at the top of a list of high-value Germans captured at its end. Held under house arrest by the Russians for a number of months, they both supposedly died from typhoid the day before their scheduled interrogation by NKVD (the KGB of the period). When the NKVD went looking for the bodies, the bodies had already mysteriously disappeared. When the Soviet intelligence officers tortured a close associate of the Rohde's, they were able to locate the general area of where the supposedly deceased couple may have been buried. They quickly mounted an all-out search scouring the area. Finally, after several days of digging, they located their caskets which were easily identified because their names were emblazoned on the wooden lids. And when the caskets were opened, they were empty. Possibly someone had stolen the bodies. Or maybe, they were never buried in the caskets at all. It could be surmised that the couple even faked their deaths. The only thing the NKVD found was a crudely carved wooden cross, about a foot long by six inches wide, placed neatly in each casket."

Jim looked to the Monsignor for any sign of recollection. The man yawned, as he looked at his watch then looked at Jim holding up two fingers indicating Jim had two minutes left. Jim continued. "In 1946, the doctor who signed the death certificates of the Rohde's disappeared before the NKVD could question him. In the Doctor's office they found a crudely carved wooden cross, about a foot long by six inches wide, placed neatly upon his desk. The same type of cross that was found in the caskets. It was as if someone was teasing the Soviets. And the doctor, he was never to be found alive."

Jim pulled another sheet of paper from his folder. "Let's jump to the year 1987. There was a famous myth debunker and treasure hunter of international reputation named, Georg Stein. The man was also famous for solving numerous cases involving old Nazis and discovering if they had survived the war and were in hiding under false names. He even worked for the Israeli government for a while, hunting down old Nazis. He went on to publish a few well-regarded books, and even do some TV specials on the subject. But in the end, the famous Mr. Stein had his enemies. Some were Nazi sympathizers, and some, according to my well-placed sources, were high ranking Vatican officials." Jim looked up from his notes, staring at the Monsignor to await his response.

"That's enough, young man," said the Monsignor in an angry tone. "How dare you implicate this office in one of your mad treasure schemes." He rose from behind his desk and walked over to his office door, opening it. "Out."

Jim ignored the Monsignor as he continued. "Someone murdered Mr. Stein after he purportedly said he finally found damning information on what had happened to the Amber Room." Jim looked up to the Monsignor, the Monsignor looked worried at this point. "I'd close that if I were you. That is unless you want others to know what happened?"

The Monsignors face appeared a ghostly white. "Are you threatening me? Or the Vatican?" he said, before wisely closing the door.

Jim smiled. "I guess I'm getting an extension on my five minutes?"

The Monsignor resumed his spot behind his desk, sitting heavily in his chair. "What do you think? Now continue with your blasphemy. Let's hear the rest of your theory."

Jim continued. "Mr. Stein not only knew what happened to the Amber Room, he even knew its location. And let's not stop there, he even knew who ordered its theft. All roads leading to this little city where we sit. Now, several hours before Mr. Stein was to appear on a Munich newscast, a newscast where he was going to reveal to the world the Amber Rooms whereabouts, he was found dead and naked, in the middle of a forest in Bavaria, Germany, his stomach cut open by a scalpel. A crudely carved wooden cross, about a foot long by six inches wide, was laid neatly upon his chest."

The Monsignor nodded. "So you think you solved the Amber Room theft. Or your Mr. Stein solved it many years ago. How come no one has come forward in all this time? That's a lot of money to leave on the table."

Jim nodded once more. "Someone did come forward," he paused, looking at the Monsignor to monitor his expression when he provided him with the name. "I am sure that you knew him well. It was one of your Vatican Intelligence Agents, Antonio Perluci."

The Monsignors eyes narrowed. "Perluci was a renegade. He never had the blessing of the Vatican for his mischievous deeds."

Jim laughed aloud. "Mischievous deeds?" he replied. "Is that what you call it? Well your little pit bull had a change of heart during his last year of life. Perluci informed my friends of every detail of the Amber Room theft before he disappeared in the Florida Keys several months ago. And he of all people should know, he organized the whole theft back in 1944. He even organized the deaths of the people I just spoke about; the Rohde's, the doctor who supposedly performed their autopsy, and let's not forget Georg Stein. Each time he left a little cross to torment any pursuers."

Jim's last words hung in the air for several moments, like a dagger ready to strike its victim.

The Monsignor smiled at him. *"So you do know."*

THE VATICAN'S FINAL SECRET by FRANCIS JOSEPH SMITH

CHAPTER 43

Present Day - Tel Aviv, Mossad HQ

Benny Machaim rose from behind his desk, walking around
it to greet Jim Dieter, Jim's hand extended; Benny pushed
it away and grabbed him in a bear hug. "You are a
welcome friend here, Jim," Benny said, smiling, 'you get a
different greeting than the rest of the usual people who
enter this office." As head of Mossad, Israeli intelligence,
Benny could have chosen to have his subordinate, Moshe
Eisen, handle Jim's request. But he would not hear it. Ever
since Jim and his fiancé, Nora Robinson, had helped them
eliminate some Nazi leftovers from the war and deliver the
diamonds back to their rightful owner or in the case of
most, their heirs, he was what they call in Israel *an ever-
welcome guest.*

Benny motioned to a chair in front of his desk.
"Please, sit," he said. Benny reached for his cell phone,

dialing a number from memory. "Moshe, our special friend, Jim Dieter, is here." After he hung up he placed the cell phone back on his desk, sitting in the chair beside Jim. "Do you mind? I want my assistant Moshe to be in on our conversation."

"Are you kidding me? Moshe is always welcome."

After several moments, a slight knock at the door is heard. Moshe opened the door slightly.

Benny waved him in. "Moshe, you remember our special friend, Jim Dieter?"

Moshe presented the same greeting as Benny, brushing aside Jim's hand and plying him with a crushing bear hug. "It's good to see you, my friend," he said.

"Jim is here because of the Monsignor," Benny began, looking first to Moshe then to Jim.

Jim looked shocked. "How did you know? I just made an appointment yesterday with your secretary saying I would like a meeting. Nothing was said. Nothing implied."

"James Dieter, what kind of organization do you think I run here?" Benny said with a smile, sounding slightly irritated. "I even know the reason you are here."

Jim shook his head. "You never cease to amaze me, Benny," he said with a wide grin.

"I will take that as a complement. Now let's get down to the reason why you are here. Or shall we say for whom you are here? Did the Monsignor send you?"

It was Jim's turn to smile.

That's all the confirmation Benny required as he continued. "That bastard. Let me tell you a few things about him. He is the lowest of the low. We have a folder on him that would make your head spin. Crooked as the day is long is an old-fashioned saying you Americans like to use."

Jim nodded in agreement. "He basically said that he wouldn't help me. Most of what I had said to him were lies and he would not provide me the dignity of an answer."

Benny looked around his office, thinking for a moment. 'Do you feel like taking a walk? It's a beautiful sunny day outside. I know after a long flight I like to exercise a bit. Does the legs some good."

Jim and Moshe both nodded. *How do you turn down a request from the head of Israeli intelligence?*

Once outside they headed across the Aluf Meir Amit Boulevard to the olive groves. Benny preferred to walk amongst the olive trees when given the chance. It allowed him a chance to relax a bit given his stressful position.

Benny nodded to Moshe, signaling for him to take over the conversation. "From what was asked of me by Benny, I have done some digging on the Pope during WWII, Pope Pius XII."

Jim looked at Benny. "How did you know the subject?"

"Benny smiled. "Allow Moshe to provide the details on what we have found." He once again nodded to Moshe.

Moshe continued. "Let's start with the basics and a quick summarization. Pope Pius XII was in pursuit of absolute power for himself and the Catholic Church so he helped Adolf Hitler destroy German Catholic political opposition, betrayed the Jews of Europe, and sealed a deeply cynical pact."

Jim looked to Benny, then back to Moshe. "That's one hell of a summarization."

"But the truth," said Benny holding up his index finger to emphasize the point.

Moshe continued. "Before he was Pope Pius XII he was known as Cardinal Pacelli. So for most of our discussion I will refer to him as Pacelli. As for my sources, I called upon our people in Europe to scour files relating to Pacelli's activities in Germany during the 1920s and 1930s, focusing on his dealings with Adolf Hitler from 1933 to 1945. The evidence was explosive. It showed for the first time that Pacelli was, by the proof of his own words, anti-Jewish. It revealed that he had helped Hitler rise to power and at the same time undermined potential Catholic resistance in Germany. Resistance that, if Pacelli had called upon it, could have stopped Hitler. It also showed that he had denied or at times trivialized the Holocaust, despite having reliable knowledge of its true magnitude. And, worse, that he was a hypocrite, for after the war he took credit for speaking out boldly against the Nazis' persecution of the Jews."

Benny pointed to several large rocks under the shade of the many olive trees surrounding them, motioning for them to sit. "Moshe has much to tell. It's better if we relax as he does."

Moshe continued. "Now, let's regress a bit. Pacelli had been recruited as a young lawyer into the Vatican in 1901, at the age of 24, to specialize in council affairs and church law. The reason he was invited was due to his father being a respected Vatican lawyer for many years. Once in the Vatican, Pacelli collaborated on the reformulation of church law called the Code of Canon Law. It was something distributed in 1917 to Catholic bishops and clergy throughout the world. This is where it gets interesting. It's as though he knew he would be Pope someday and was setting himself up for a coup. What did he do? He helped rewrite Canon Law. His revisions would basically state that all future bishops would be nominated by the Pope; heresy would not be tolerated; priests would be subjected to strict censorship in their writings; papal letters to the faithful would be regarded as infallible; and an oath would be taken by all priests to submit to the strict doctrine laid down by the Pope. More than any other Vatican official of the century, Pacelli promoted the idea of papal control, the highly centralized, dictatorial authority he himself assumed on March 2, 1939, and maintained until his death in October 1958."

Jim was the first to speak. "It's a dictatorship. Whatever I say goes."

Benny nodded. "This is the second time I am hearing this. And its gets more disturbing each time."

Moshe also nodded in agreement. "But there was a problem in Germany. The church had historically granted the archdioceses in the states of Germany a large measure of freedom from Rome. The main reason was due to Germany having one of the largest Catholic populations in the world. The historic autonomy of Germanys Catholic

Church was protected in ancient church-state treaties known as concordats. Onward seventeen years and already an archbishop, Pacelli was sent to Munich to start the process of eliminating all existing legal challenges to the new papal authority. At the same time, he was to pursue a Reich Concordat, a treaty between the papacy and Germany that would supersede all local agreements. A Reich Concordat would mean formal recognition by the German government of the Popes right to impose the new Code of Canon Law on Germanys Catholics."

Jim looked to Benny. "He was ..."

Benny finished his sentence for him. "Setting himself up to be Pope."

Jim looked perplexed. "How come no one has addressed this before?"

"Is this the type of news you would want to hear if you control one of the world's largest religions?" said Benny. "But as interesting as that was, Moshe is ready to drop the bomb. Please continue, Moshe."

Moshe smiled before he continued. "After Hitler came to power in January 1933, he made the concordat discussions with Pacelli a priority. The negotiations ensued over six months with constant shuttle diplomacy between the Vatican and Berlin. Hitler spent more time on this treaty than on any other item of foreign diplomacy during his short tenure. In the end, Hitler insisted that his signature on the concordat would depend on the Catholic aligned Parties voting for the Enabling Act, the legislation that was to give him dictatorial powers. Pacelli agreed, telling his followers to vote for the Enabling Act, which they evidently did. After the Reich Concordat was signed,

Pacelli collaborated in the withdrawal of German Catholics from political and social activity."

Jim couldn't believe what he had just heard. "He basically sold out the German people and allowed Hitler to rise to power. He set up the basis for World War II."

Benny looked around the olive grove, the sun was just reaching its peak overhead. "I prefer to say that he allowed a cold blooded murderer to assume power. And many of my people paid the price for his power move. But again, let Moshe finish. More interesting information is coming."

Moshe nodded. "On February 10, 1939, Pius XI died. Pacelli, then 63, was elected by the College of Cardinals to succeed him. He was crowned on March 12, the day before Hitler's march into Prague. The following month, at Pacelli's urging, the Vatican's ambassador in Berlin, hosted a reception in honor of Hitler's 50th birthday. A birthday greeting to the *Führer* from the bishops of Germany would become an annual tradition until the wars end. As Europe plunged toward war, Pacelli continued to seek to pacify Hitler by attempting to persuade the Poles to make concessions over Germany's territorial claims. After Hitler's invasion of Poland, on September 1, 1939, he declined to denounce Germany."

The smile had long left Benny's face. In a serious tone, he said: "Let me repeat that for you. The head of the Catholic Church declined to denounce Germany's actions. They just started World War II and the pompous little shit wouldn't even say boo to the man." Benny rose from the small boulder he was sitting on, pacing amongst the olives trees, tears streaming down his face.

Moshe leaned in to Jim. In a low voice, he said: "Benny lost over half of his family in Poland. Most at Auschwitz."

Benny used his sleeve to wipe the tears from his eyes before turning back to take his seat. "Pardon me but I tend to get more emotional with each passing year." He waved his hand at Moshe to continue.

"We move forward three years to September 1942, when your President Franklin Roosevelt sent his personal representative to plead with Pacelli to make a statement about the extermination of the Jews, handing him a dossier replete with information on the Jewish mass killings in hopes that the Pope would condemn the Nazi regime. Of course, nothing happened. But what finally caused Pacelli to make a move against Hitler? One that Hitler would never know about? When Pacelli found out that Hitler had a plan to forcefully remove the Pope and take the Vatican treasures to Liechtenstein. The SS commander in Italy warned Hitler that such an attempt to invade the Vatican and its properties, or to seize the Pope, would prompt a severe backlash throughout Italy."

"Although Hitler backed down, the news made it to Pacelli and he wanted to strike back at Hitler. But how? This is when synchronicity raised its ugly head. The very day he heard of Hitler's plan, one of his papal intelligence agents working in Prussia discovered the presence of the Amber Room. And that's not all. It was being stored in a church basement. A Catholic Church basement. *Synchronicity*. Now Pacelli decided to act. He tasked one of his most trusted agents, someone with whom you were first adversaries with, then friends; one Antonio Perluci.

Of course Pacelli knew Perluci was ruthless and just the person to help him steal the Amber Room right from under the Nazis. And apparently, that's what he accomplished."

With the stories conclusion, Benny stood up and walked over to Moshe, he placed his hand on top of his shoulder, before he turned to Jim. "This man has a photographic memory. He read that report three times and was able to memorize every detail. You can see why he is my deputy."

Jim nodded. "Sounds like I came to the right place after all."

"Of course you did. So now you have The Vatican, the Hezbollah, and God knows who else after you. Sounds like you could use a friend." With that, Benny pulled out his cell phone and turned away to walk amongst the olive groves. Moshe and Jim overheard only parts of the conversation; Jim thought it was in Latin.

After several moments, Benny returned. "The wheels are in motion," he said.

CHAPTER 44

Present Day – Vatican City

The Monsignor shook his head at seeing Jim in his anteroom. "I thought you promised me you would never bother me again?" He rolled his eyes in jest as he signaled for Jim to come into his office. "I take it that Benny provided you with answers to your questions?"

"I wouldn't be here unless he did."

"Benny and I never could see eye-to-eye. He tends to think we, the Vatican, are hiding information from him about fabulous treasures."

Jim smiled at his take on things.

"See. Your smile says it all. Why would the Vatican want to become involved with the theft of the Nazi held, Russian owned, Amber Room?" the Monsignor queried in a tone as though it were a minor effort. "Why would we want such a colossal beast?"

Jim shook his head. "Perluci told me himself. Hell, he even drove the truck to these very gates. All under the direct orders of Pope Pius XII. Then I also received my confirmation from Benny. He has nothing to gain. You even directed me towards him."

The Monsignor's face was flush. "Perluci was a rogue agent," he said. "He tended to take matters into his own hands and not ask his superiors for guidance. If you had any dealings with the man you know I speak the truth."

"If you remember your history correctly, just a few months ago your office let Perluci and his crew loose on me," said Jim. Of course he was referring to when the Vatican Special Operations Group, of which Perluci was one of its top agents, went after Jim and Dan for the Nazi Gold Train proceeds. Eventually Perluci turned and sided with Jim and Dan. "So speak the truth now. Why did the Vatican steal the Amber Room?"

The Monsignor smiled as he reached for a hand-carved wooden box on his desk, opening it, he pulled out a cigarette, offering one to Jim, who declined. "Nasty habit, I only smoke when my nerves require calming."

"Obviously, this is one of those times."

The Monsignor nodded as he lit the cigarette. He puffed a few times, picking a piece of tobacco from his tongue and flicking it towards the floor. It seemed to have the desired effect as he leaned back in his chair, and grinned. "So all of the information you have heard to date has come from two sources, Perluci and Benny?" He did not look at Jim; he already had his confirmation. He blew smoke rings up towards the ceiling. Let me tell you something about those two, they are both liars and cheats. It is what they do for a living."

Jim laughed aloud, "And you are any different? Give me a break."

The Monsignor rose from his chair, walking over to his window fronting St. Peter's Square. His back was to Jim.

Jim used the moment to glance at the two iPhones he had stowed in his jacket pockets, one provided an open phone line, the others sole purpose to record the conversation.

"Only people of high importance have a view like this," he said, his hand taking in the wide expanse. "They," he began pointing over towards the Popes residence, "have entrusted me with all of the state secrets." He took another puff on his cigarette before he walked back to his desk and extinguished it in a glass ashtray sitting on top. He stayed standing, looking down on Jim as he stood there. "I will tell you something. And it's something you will want to hear. I can guarantee you will not hear something like this again. I've performed a lot of research on the subject utilizing documents you will never see. Documents so secret, only myself and maybe 11 others have been privy to its contents."

The Monsignor paused for several seconds as if contemplating what he was about to say; or if he should even continue. "You are right. During the War, the Pope did nothing. He basically bowed down to Hitler and all of his cronies. He should have spoken up and denounced *the little paperhanger*. If he did Hitler would never have been elected to office in Germany. He would have been a minor official with an axe to grind. The Pope missed his chance, and because of it, probably allowed World War II to happen."

Jim sat up a little straighter in his chair, hoping his phone was still recording.

The Monsignor continued. "The Pope realized in 1944 that he had truly screwed up. But what was he to do about it? He wanted to strike Hitler were it would hurt the most: his pocketbook. He authorized Perluci to go after the Amber Room. He knew it was Hitler's pride and joy. Something Hitler had stolen from under the very nose of Stalin, his archrival. Now Pope Pius had the opportunity to do the same to him."

He walked over to the window once more, a smile graced his face as if it were the last time he would see the Square in all its majesty. "Perluci went to the city of Königsberg hoping to make contact with Dr. Rohde, the curator of the Königsberg Castle and where the Germans had kept the Amber Room stored. Perluci went to work at the same church Dr. Rohde was known to frequent. Little did he know that Rohde was looking for a place to store the Amber Room and protect it from the Allied bombing attacks. Under the disguise of a priest he was able to placate Rohde and have him store the treasure in the church's basement. That was allowing the fox to watch the chickens. Once stored in the basement, Perluci, like any thief, managed to steal what he could. He drove it back here and today it is stored in our Vatican Secret Vaults. Specifically, our Red Badge area." He walked back over to his desk. "So now you know the true story."

Jim sat smiling. "I thank you for the truth. No," he said as he held up both of his iPhones for the Monsignor to see, "the world thanks you for your honesty."

A look of shock spread across the Monsignors face. "And I thought we were operating under the flag of trust," he said, shaking his head. He slowly reached down to open his desk drawer, and pulled out a 38 revolver, bringing the weapon to bear on Jim. "Believe me," he said, "I know how to use this."

"Of that I have no doubt," replied Jim calmly. "Why don't you just put the weapon on the desk and we can talk this out."

"The talking part is long done. You have your information. When that recording about the Amber Room leaks out, I'm a dead man," replied the Monsignor.

"What do you mean you're a dead man? Who's going to kill you?"

The Monsignor pointed across the Square, "They will," he said, before he looked down at the gun and then Jim. "Well there is only one way to end this. Either you die and nobody hears what you have recorded on your phone, or" he paused for several seconds, "I get disgraced. And then somebody kills me."

"Let me make it easier for you," replied Jim, holding up the phone, showing it to the Monsignor, I have been recording on one phone and," he held up the other phone with the open line, "Benny has been on the line with us the whole time. Say hello, Benny."

""Shalom, Monsignor," said Benny from the comfort of his Tel Aviv office. "It's been long time since we last talked."

The Monsignor knew he was outplayed, still he pointed the 38 up and down several times at Jim. "May I see the both of you in Hell," he said at the top of his voice as he turned the weapon on himself. He smiled at Jim as he placed the 38 in his mouth and pulled the trigger, a deafening blast rocked the small room.

Jim had jumped up from his seat as the Monsignor turned the gun on himself, but it was already too late, the body had dropped to the floor with a soft thud.

Jim looked down at the now dead Monsignor. "Benny, you were right about him. It's a shame he will never know what really happened to the Amber Room."

CHAPTER 45

October 1944 Vipiteno, Italy

Perluci easily navigated the streets of Vipiteno on his return to *Our Lady of the Marsh Church*. He drove the truck to the back garage, honking once, one of the carpenters opened the doors in response. Once safely inside, he marveled at the carpenters work on the crates. With their work complete, carpenters sat on the side eating some cheese and drinking red wine.

Perluci stepped down, a wide grin on his face. "You have done well in my absence he said to the lead brother.

"Grazie, grazie," replied the brother in Italian. "Where is the gentleman that you were with this morning?" he said just as Father Stefano walked in, closing the door behind him.

"Yes," said Father Stefano, "where is our escort?"

Perluci had anticipated as much. "I left him at the other Church. I'm going to pick him up after I load the crates these fine gentlemen built."

The brothers beamed at the praise, secretly hoping a bonus was in order.

Father Stefano stared hard at Perluci, his eyes narrowed. "You left him there to do what?" he asked, his tone sardonic.

"I left him there to do what I asked him to do," he replied, the smile from his face now removed. Perluci still needed the priest to accomplish several jobs for him. The last thing he needed now was a difficult subordinate. "He is a good worker who follows orders," he said, before turning his attention back to the carpenters. "I see you even spray painted the crates with the Nazi emblem. Good, very good," he said as he walked around the crates. When he finished his inspection he withdrew a stack of Lira from his pocket, counting out 60,000 before handing it to the older brother.

"No, sir," he protested meekly, "it is too much. We agreed on 30,000 Lira."

Perluci shook his head. "I am giving you a small bonus plus I require some additional work from you and your brother. That is the reason for my paying double. I require the crates to be stuffed with cheap artwork. The cheaper the better." He walked over to the crate that the carpenters had used as their example, opening the lid with a borrowed hammer. Once open he motioned for the men to look inside. "I need paintings to occupy the same space and have about the same weight." He pointed for them to lift the crate.

"Yes, sir," the older one replied. "We can find art work of the same weight to fill your crates."

Perluci grinned. "He handed them an additional 30,000 Lira. "Whatever you save out of the 30,000 Lira, you can keep for yourselves."

Both brothers took turns in shaking his hand for his generosity. "We know of just the shop. It is located in a small village only five kilometers from here. We will have your crates filled with the artwork you requested. We could be done in two hours' time."

Perluci admired the men. Or was it their greed? So similar to his own. "Thank-you," he said, "that would be perfect."

One job down and one more to go.

CHAPTER 46

Present Day - The Vatican, Italy

The Vatican spokesman confidently strode to the podium, a determined look upon his face. He shuffled his notes as he lay them down upon the podium. News had already leaked of an overhaul within the Vatican's hierarchy of operations that signaled a troubled period in the Popes' papacy.

In the leaked document, it was stated that five Cardinals, ten Bishops, and numerous subordinates had resigned effective immediately. The Pope had already accepted their resignations. But everyone was aware they really hadn't resigned; *they were fired*. But why the sudden firings? This was why over 30 reporters had gathered on only one hours' notice.

It was something unprecedented in all of the Vatican's reign.

The spokesman tapped the podiums microphone a few times to get the room to settle down. After several attempts, the room finally quieted. "At this time of transition in Vatican leadership, we think it's best the Holy Father is completely free to assemble a new team," he began.

A women reporter interrupted him with a shout: "What happened to the Head of Vatican Secret Archives, Monsignor Canti La Russo?" she yelled.

Another voice was heard asking why an ambulance and a medical examiner were called to the Vatican yesterday.

"Was it murder?" shouted yet another.

"Please, please," said the spokesman in frustration as he held up his notes. "Your questions will all be answered in due time if you allow me to finish."

He waited until the room had quieted once more before he continued. "Over the course of the past 24 hours we have had a major shakeup of our most senior Vatican staff. As of this morning, the Holy Father has asked for and accepted the resignation of his five most senior Cardinals, ten Bishops, and over 20 of their subordinates. The resignations effective immediately."

The room came alive once more, questions being shouted, reporters all jostling each other trying to get the best angle for their cameras.

The spokesman looked to his aide in disgust, the aide merely shrugging his shoulders. He decided to keep speaking over the crowd. "They were asked to resign due to their connection in the death of Monsignor Canti La Russo, the Head of Vatican Secret Archives. Or formally the head of."

The room started to fall silent as he continued to speak.

"Monsignor Canti La Russo committed suicide in his office. His death was attributed to a cover-up at the Vatican's highest levels due to something that transpired during WWII."

Again, the room came alive, questions being shouted at breakneck speed.

Tears were running down the cheeks of the spokesman, obviously a dear friend of the Monsignor who had committed suicide. His aide walked to the podium, him providing a smile in reassurance as he gently removed the notes from the spokesman's hands. The aide now stood staring at the reporters, him not saying a word as he waited for them to settle down. After several minutes, the reporters realized nothing would be forthcoming unless they were to maintain order amongst themselves. They realized this would be the top story of the year, possibly the decade. *Why would a Pope ask for the resignation of all of his staff?* It had never been done in all of years of the papacy.

The room went quiet once more. The aide smiled at the assembled reporters. "I assume that most of you might be acquainted with the eighth wonder of the world, the Amber Room."

The reporters started talking in a hushed tone amongst themselves.

"The Amber Room was built by Kings and Queens to be admired by Kings and Queens. It was a golden room completely bedecked in floor-to-ceiling amber, gold, and semiprecious stones. The room today is worth anywhere from $200 million to ½ a billion. This treasure was highly prized by Hitler. So he made it a prime target of his invading Armies and stole it from the Soviets during WWII. The Nazis put it on display for several years until it mysteriously disappeared. And depending on your source, it was either destroyed during an Allied bombing raid, sunk on a German hospital ship fleeing Königsberg, or destroyed unintentionally by Soviet Artillery."

"Well, for the first time in public, the Vatican is announcing that we actually rescued the Amber Room during WWII and for its safekeeping, had it placed down in our Vatican Secret Vaults." He turned to the spokesman, the man having composed himself, and relinquished the podium to him.

The spokesman held his hands aloft in an attempt to quiet the room. At the same time, ten Pontifical Swiss Guards dressed in their traditional red, yellow and blue fanciful uniforms, filed into the room as they marched into place behind the spokesman.

Suddenly, with the arrival of the Swiss Guards, the room became eerily quiet. As the reporters looked from the podium to their fellow reporters, it became abundantly clear what was about to be revealed. Then, in walked the Pope, a bleak look upon his face. He stood behind the spokesman, them talking in a low voice for several minutes before the spokesman graciously moved aside to allow His Holiness the podium.

The Pope managed a weak smile to the assembled reporters before speaking: "I could not allow in good conscious someone to make an excuse for something that was done by one of my predecessors so long ago. Whatever the intent of Pope Pius XII during World War II, he should have returned the Amber Room back to its rightful owners, what was then known as the Soviet Union, now Russia, after the war. I am about to right a wrong that until 24 hours ago I never knew existed. And yes, this is the reason why I have asked for and accepted the resignations of my staff. As of tomorrow we will be in discussions to return the Amber Room to the Russian government and eventually to its rightful home at the Catherine Palace. These gentlemen behind me," pointing to the Swiss Guards, "will now take each of you down to a place very few people have had the privilege of entering, the Vatican Vaults; there you will see for yourself why the Amber Room was once called the eighth wonder of the world."

Reporters were all calling their editors, begging for live airtime. *This was the story of the century.*

CHAPTER 47

October 1944 Vipiteno, Italy

True to their word, the carpenters returned in just under two hours' time, their truck full of worthless paintings, careful to have only purchased sizes that would fit in the crates. They backed their truck up to the garage door ready to unload their cargo.

Upon hearing the truck enter the driveway, Perluci and Father Stefano walked over from the church in time to see the truck already against the door. The two brothers jumped out of their truck slapping their hands together in self-congratulations. They obviously made a good deal with the shopkeeper in the next village.

The oldest brother removed the hat from his head when Father Stefano approached him, holding it in his hands. "Good evening, Father," he said, a wide grin upon his face. "We were able to buy everything you needed and still make a tidy sum for ourselves." He looked over to his brother, him nodding and smiling in return. "Thanks to the two of you we should have enough money put away to last the remainder of the war."

"We were glad to help," replied Father Stefano. "But remember, you can't tell a soul about what transpired here."

The man nodded in reassurance. "The paintings we bought off an old friend who deals with the local black market. We said nothing about our customer and he didn't ask. As far as the wood for the crates, my Aunt owns a sawmill. You pay her in cash, she doesn't ask questions.

Father Stefano smiled. He was well aware of the local Mafia, trying to avoid any unnecessary entanglements with them. "Now we need you to unload your truck and pack the crates. Once that is complete, load the crates onto the German truck. This man," pointing to Perluci, "must be on the road tonight."

"But load the sample crate last," shot back Perluci. He needed that crate in the right position for the next and final phase of his operation.

"Yes," said the eldest with an all-knowing grin. "Like I said, we have dealt with the Mafia all our lives. I understand what you are doing."

Perluci instinctively tapped his shoulder holster. "And I will need the two of you to leave your truck here and accompany me for my ride to Rome. There is an extra 30,000 Lira in it for you. You can catch a train back when I am done with you."

The eldest spoke. "We need to be back by tomorrow night. We have work around our small farm that we can't neglect."

"One way or another, you will be home tomorrow," Perluci said. "Now get this done so we can stay on schedule." Perluci then walked off to the church. He had a phone call to make.

The oldest looked to his brother. They each winked at the other. There was something about Perluci they didn't trust. That was the main reason for stopping off at their farm before returning, each grabbing their American 38 calibers, gifts of a grateful Mafioso who they had helped before the war."

One way or another, somebody was going to be rich in a few hours.

CHAPTER 48

Present Day - Vatican City - The Vatican Vaults

The Vatican Vaults are not public—and at one time where only accessible to scholars once they reached the ripe old age of 75 years old—and even then underwent a thorough vetting process.

However, in recent years the Vatican has become a bit more relaxed with its secrets. In 2012, the Vatican Secret Archives even displayed a public exhibition of some of its more prominent documents.

But that minor moment of openness contradicted the real secrets still hidden in the archival treasure trove. *And that included everything dated after 1939 still closed to the public, including the papers of Pope Pius XII, whose silence during the World War II has been interpreted as collaboration with Hitler.* Though the church has released certain documents it considers favorable to Pius XII, it refuses to release them all.

And nothing from the Red Badge Area has ever been released for viewing.

****

FIVE VATICANS GUARDS stood guard outside the lone elevator leading to the subterranean Vatican's Secret Archives. The sergeant-at-arms confirmed the identity of each person holding a Press credential to an overall master security list. Once approved they were allowed, seven at a time, to enter the elevator and descend down five stories to the Archives. When they reached the bottom floor the elevator doors opened to reveal yet an additional seven Vatican Guards awaiting them. Here, each of the Press were assigned a Vatican guard who conducted a final body search for any electronic devices, including cameras.

All of their reporting would be accomplished the old fashioned way: *by taking notes*.

After their final inspection, they stepped into the brightly lit corridor afforded them just outside the Vatican Vaults. Impressive just to gaze at, the glass fronted, vacuum-sealed room housed almost forty thousand volumes on miles of shelving, containing over thirteen centuries worth of documents. But in the very back of the room lay the even more restrictive Red Badge area. As they looked on from the corridor, they could see the Pope near the Red Badge Room. He looked to be giving orders to three of the Vatican Guards, each with metal hand trucks. In a matter of minutes the Guards and the Pope were in the corridor with three wooden crates, the Nazi swastika still stenciled eerily on the crates sides reminding those gathered of the circuitous route the crates had undertaken.

The Pope instructed the Vatican Guards nearest him to open the first crate. In a matter of seconds the six nails were pried out, the lid now off. Two of the guards removed white gloves from their pockets and placed them on their hands. After a nod from the Pope, they gingerly pulled up the first panel. At the halfway point, they were greeted by a series of oohs and ah's from the Press, each able to view the panels sheer beauty.

The Pope smiled at the assembled crowd. "You can see why we would want to save the Amber Room from certain destruction." He walked over to a panel being held by one of the Vatican Guards and touched the amber facing. "Absolutely beautiful."

The Press was sold for the moment. But how it would play out in the media tomorrow was another story.

"Besides these three crates, there are an additional twenty more in the Red Badge Room," said the Pope. "I hope to have the Russian Ambassador visit tonight so she can view something no Russian has seen in almost 80 years."

The Pope pointed to the other crates. "Open those also. We have nothing to hide. Let our guests see what we have protected."

CHAPTER 49

October 1944 Vipiteno, Italy

Darkness had set in. The truck was packed and ready to go, its engine idling. Two small Vatican flags flew from the right and left hand sides of the trucks hood. The Vatican flag was also painted on top of the truck in case of an aircraft spotting them in day light. In the back of the truck paper Vatican flags were glued over the Nazi emblems. They were ready. Up in the truck's cab sat the two brothers in the passenger and middle seats awaiting Perluci's return; he had just excused himself and ran into the church to see Father Stefano.

Perluci waited until he was out of view of the brothers in the truck before he withdrew his pistol. He couldn't afford to leave any witnesses. He slowly opened the door leading into the churches kitchen, the last place they had seen Father Stefano. There he sat, alone, reading his bible, drinking a cup of ersatz coffee. He looked up as Perluci slowly walked in, gun raised.

"You have come to finish the job, haven't you?" he said in resignation. "I was expecting you. That's why I stayed here to make it easier for you."

Perluci looked around the kitchen.

"Don't worry, I gave the maid the night off. It's just you and I."

Perluci walked over to the Priest, his gun leading the way. "You understand I can't have witnesses in my line of work?"

"I understand. You must do, what you must do. Get on with it. Shoot me. I have nothing to fear," he said as he adjusted his reading glasses. "My conscience, unlike yours, is clear."

Perluci gradually lowered his weapon. He couldn't kill the man. There was something about him that reminded Perluci of his own father. Maybe it was his 'do as you must' attitude. Perluci holstered his weapon. "Can I count on your discretion to keep my secret about the crates?"

"My son, I have been chosen for this posting solely due to my ability to keep its secrets. It's not me you have to worry about. But someone else."

Perluci shot him a quick glance. "Don't play games with me old man. What the hell are you talking about?"

"As I said, I have been chosen due to my ability to keep secrets. You'll find out in due time."

Perluci reached for his weapon but thought better of it. "I just ask that you keep my secret."

Father Stefano simply nodded.

Perluci nodded in return.

"Remember, you have to be in the town of Remi by 0700 hours," said Father Stefano. "It's right on the front lines. There is a scheduled truce between the German Army and the Americans for only two hours. They agreed to clear the battlefield of the wounded soldiers before they start the senseless killing again. It is the only time you will be able to get through the lines until something like this happens again. Our people in Vatican City have contacted the governments in Berlin and Washington to make them aware a Vatican truck with important Vatican documents will be passing through the lines. You should have no issues with your diplomatic papers and the Vatican flags. It all depends on what type of soldiers you run across. But you should be allowed through."

"It doesn't sound too reassuring."

"Life never is," replied Father Stefano.

Perluci then left the same way he had come in. He scrambled across the yard towards the idling truck. For the first time in his life he let someone live who, by all rights, should have been killed. At least under the old Perluci rules. He merely shook his head as he climbed up into the truck's cab knowing he had two more people to deal with. And soon.

No questions asked.

CHAPTER 50

0655hrs - Remi, Italy - October 1944

Perluci had driven the entire journey, covering the 310 kilometers in just under 10 hours. Not bad with a war on. It aided them that the Auto Stradia was basically devoid of cars at the time they drove, between that and the lack of petrol. Also, with luck on their side, they were able to attach themselves to a small, 10 truck German Army convoy, which allowed them to bypass the customary military checkpoints.

Entering the town of Remi with five minutes to spare before the truce went into effect they viewed utter devastation. Not a single building standing had a roof or window. What the Allied artillery had missed, German demolition teams had destroyed. Now the retreating Germans tried to destroy what they had missed in their "scorched earth" retreat from the town. The town had no communications, transportation, water, or power grid. The Germans even mined the remaining buildings, and tore up railroad tracks that had once gone through the center of town. The town, originally with just under 5,000 inhabitants before the war, was lucky to contain 50. With most taking refuge in their basement, the only part of their homes still capable of sustaining them. Black bunting hung from most doorways signifying they were in mourning from a lost relative.

As Perluci drove the truck, he was waved through town by German Army police on the only road still capable of bearing traffic. Obviously the local commanders were informed of their approach. At the edge of town a German Army Police Captain signaled for his men to stop Perluci's truck; they responded by rolling 50 gallon barrels in his path. When the truck halted, the Captain jumped up on the truck's driver side running board.

Perluci immediately grasped by the man's impeccable camouflaged uniform that he was not a combat soldier, but of the notorious SS. He looked like he had just stepped off a SS recruiting poster: 6 foot tall, blond, blue eyed.

He leaned in the driver's side window to confront Perluci. "What is so important that this sole truck has to cross no man's land?" the Captain said, his hand sweeping the area in front of them.

Perluci smiled at the captain, not wanting to upset the man any further. He produced his diplomatic passport and handed it to him. "Here are our credentials, Captain," he said in an even tone, showing no stress. "In the back of our truck are religious items and paperwork from our various embassies. We only wish to return to Vatican City. I understand that your superiors have cleared us to our final destination."

The captain reached into his uniform pocket and pulled out the latest communiqué. He then smiled at Perluci as he pointed to the two passengers in his cab. "Where are their papers?" he said. "This piece of paper states that only you are to pass. Nothing about passengers."

"But they are my assistants," he replied. "I can't move the crates without them. My diplomatic passport should also extend to them."

The captain jumped down from the sideboard, motioning to three of his fellow SS soldiers. "Take the two passengers out," he ordered.

The carpenters looked to Perluci for help as the SS opened the passenger side door, their weapons pointed directly at them. "You must help us," they pleaded. "Please."

The SS soldier fired a short burst from his machine pistol into the air. "Now," he demanded.

Perluci made a sign of the cross to them as they each jumped down, hands in the air.

The SS captain ordered the barrels obstructing Perluci's truck removed. He then provided Perluci with a stiff armed Nazi salute. "Move along," he demanded.

Perluci shifted gears and slowly proceeded towards the American lines. In his rear view mirror he watched in horror as the SS soldiers lined up the two brothers against the remains of a brick wall, and with a long burst from their machine pistols, summarily executed them.

Perluci now turned his attention to the road in front of him, eyeing the American troops no more than 50 meters away. As he drove, a smile creased his face. He suddenly realized it was a blessing in disguise that the SS had executed the brothers.

It only saved him from the same undertaking.

CHAPTER 51

Present Day – Vatican City - Vatican Vaults

The Vatican Guards opened the next two crates. Very carefully they pulled up the second crates contents. When it was fully up and out of the crate, the room roared with laughter. The Pope turned in time to see a painting of dogs playing poker.

The Vatican Guards supervisor pushed his men out of the way, ignoring the pleas of those around him to put on white gloves, he reached in and pulled out an oil on canvas painting of an apple; a large green apple. The laughter was only getting louder as he turned to the Pope.

"Inspect the rest of the crates," ordered the Pope. Two of the Vatican Guards scrambled back into the archives; once inside they sprinted to the Red Badge area.

The guards supervisor looked to the Pope, catching his eye he mouthed the name Perluci to him. The Pope's face turned crimson red as he waited for the Vatican Guards to reveal the contents of the remaining crates.

From the corridor everyone watched in anticipation as the Guards tore open three additional crates in the rear of the archives.

In a matter of minutes everyone had their answer: *more of the same cheap paintings.*

"Perluci," screamed the typically unflappable Pope, as he raced to the elevator.

CHAPTER 52

October 1944 - Vatican City

After an additional five hours of driving, Perluci arrived in a liberated Rome, a city he had departed eight months ago to deal with the Amber Room situation. As he drove down the Viale Angelico he marveled at how the city had escaped the destruction reigned down upon the rest of Italy. The city appeared lively as he observed American and British troops mingling with the local populace, sitting in outdoor cafes, drinking, laughing. A much different scene then he experienced in the German occupied north.

Perluci dreamed of eating in his favorite restaurant, *Lucinda's*. Hopefully after he dropped off his cargo and met with his superiors he would be free to eat a decent meal for a change. There was only so much liver and pork one could eat, which was basically his steady diet in German occupied territories.

Perluci now viewed the imposing wall that surrounded the Vatican, in some places it stood 30 to 50 feet high. He bypassed the tourist entrance to St. Peter's Square and drove an additional 50 meters to the 'employee' entrance and the only gate that could accommodate an army truck the size he was driving.

Perluci was well-known among the Vatican Police who manned the gate. The guards snapped to attention as Perluci drove up and stopped at their small guardhouse.

The senior of the two guards saluted Perluci. "Sir, I have been told to wave you through. Also, the director and four men will be waiting to help you unload."

Perluci nodded before returning the salute. He drove the narrow lane afforded him, a road he was well acquainted with. In a matter of minutes, he was at the rear entrance to the Vatican Archives. He could see the director of the archives and his laborers awaiting his arrival. Perluci effortlessly backed the truck up to the loading dock.

The Director greeted him warmly. "Antonio Perluci, you have completed a job none of us thought possible."

Perluci knew a promotion was in the air. This had to be the most perilous job someone in the Vatican had ever undertaken and completed; *Alive*. He watched as the laborers opened drew back the canvas covering the trucks cargo area. He then pointed to the crate he knew to contain the only piece of the Amber Room.

"Open up that crate, please," he instructed the workmen.

The workmen looked to the Director for concurrence; he merely nodded in response.

A crowbar was produced, and after six nails were pried out of the crate, the crate lid was pushed aside. One of the men was about to heave the first Amber panel out of the box when Perluci stopped him. He turned to the Director. "If you don't mind, I would like to do it."

The Director readily agreed. "This man drove the Amber Room all the way from the Baltic Sea to here, through numerous Nazi roadblocks, through thousands of kilometers of our enemies. Get out of his way."

The workman graciously backed away.

Perluci pulled a set of white, soft leather gloves from his pocket and put them on. He was ready. Slowly he pulled the first panel up out of its home for the past several weeks.

A series of ah's greeted him as the beauty of the panel revealed itself.

"You have done us a great service, Antonio," said the Director, choosing to call him by his first name.

Perluci had to keep his ruse going. "We must keep them out of the light, Director. They are too valuable to be out here in the elements. They are so very fragile."

"Button up the crate," ordered the Director, concurring with Perluci. "All of this is to be taken below and put into the Red Badge area. They are to remain in the crates per my orders."

His ruse worked. The Vatican would keep them concealed forever knowing that putting them on display would expose their theft. Unless someone opened the crates, which he doubted, his secret would never be exposed.

He was going to be a very rich man.

CHAPTER 53

Present day - Zurich, Switzerland

Hassan Talif clutched his leather briefcase in his left hand as he walked up to a well-known diamond shop, opening its door to the sound of a little bell clanging overhead. In less than a second, a hidden camera fed his image into its facial recognition software to assess that Hassan was not a known threat. Just inside the shop a discreetly placed guard stood with a semi-automatic weapon slung low across his chest. Hassan nodded to the man as he walked up to the main glass counter displaying a variety of loose diamonds, the lowest priced at $10,000 francs, or $10,100 US.

An immaculately dressed salesman greeted him in English, "How may I be of service to you, sir," he said. "We have a variety of jewelry and diamonds to amaze any special person you may have in your life."

Hassan smiled as he placed his leather briefcase on top of the 13mm thick laminate counter.

The guard raised his weapon in response.

Hassan swiftly realized his mistake. He raised his hands to show no ill intentions. He then reached down to turn the briefcase around towards the salesman. "My apologies at getting your guard a little excited. Please be my guest and open the case."

The salesman signaled for the guard to lower his weapon. He then turned his attention back to Hassan. "You want to sell something, sir," he said.

"Oh, yes. Most definitely."

The salesman opened the briefcase, his eyes went wide, betraying the value of its contents. He looked up to Hassan with a smile on his face. "This is a lot of diamonds, sir. I haven't seen a cache of this size in a number of years. If my memory serves me correctly, there was a diamond robbery several weeks ago from a jet in Brussels. This briefcase of diamonds wouldn't have anything to do with that robbery, now would they?" The salesman made eye contact with the guard, he pointed to the door. The guard walked over to the front door and slid two bolts into place before turning over the closed sign.

Hassan could see that the negotiating was under way. "My name is Hassan Talif. I represent our mutual friends in Lebanon."

The salesman nodded. "How is the Sheik? I hear his predecessor was a victim of the Israelis. Such a shame. He was a *very* good customer."

The Sheik enjoyed presenting his many mistresses with extravagant gifts, always bringing them to this particular shop in Zurich. "Yes, he liked his diamonds," replied Hassan.

The salesman signaled to the guard to obtain refreshments. "Let's take the case over to our sitting area and we can become more comfortable as we discuss our business."

They walked over to where two distressed leather chairs sat in front of a gas fireplace. In front of the chairs was a coffee table where the salesman placed the briefcase, now closed. The salesman pushed a remote control button and the fireplace instantly sprang to life. "I like a nice comfortable setting," he said, pointing to the chair opposite of him for Hassan to sit down. The guard placed a silver tray on the coffee table containing glasses and a bottle of a very expensive cognac and a single malt scotch.

The salesman took a glass and pointed to the bottles. "Which would you prefer?"

Hassan indicated the single malt.

"I can see you have very good taste, sir. That is a $3,000 Franc bottle of Scotch." He poured one for Hassan and one for himself. "A toast to the new Sheik. May he live in good health."

Hassan raised his glass, clinking it with the salesman's.

"I can see from your expression, you like the good stuff," said the salesman. He pointed to the guard. "When we have concluded our business, I will have him put a case in your car."

"You are too kind. I'm sorry but I don't know your name."

"Anton. Anton Malseed at your service."

"Well, Anton, let us get down to business. You know whom I represent. From what I understand the people I work for have been very good customers." He reached over to touch the case. "I am willing to take 60% of the actual value of our product," he said with confidence."

"That's a large quantity of diamonds in that case. I will have to have each one recut to hide its original identity. That will cost me a lot of money." He reached over to grab the scotch, refilling Hassan's glass and then his own. "A lot of money," he repeated.

Hassan could see which way the number was going and it wasn't moving in his favor.

"Due to the product we have here being very hot at the moment, the most I could offer you would be 20%."

Hassan slammed his glass down on the table. "You must be joking," he said. "I consider that an insult."

"And I still have to verify that the diamonds are of good quality to even offer you that price."

"Would you insult the Sheik like this?"

"I'd insult my own mother if she brought me a brief case full of hot diamonds. Business is business."

Anton poured more scotch in Hassan's glass hoping to sooth him. "Let me take the brief case to the back room and run some tests. I would like to see what grade we are talking about. If its clarity grade of 1 or 2 for most of the lot I might be able to move my number up to 30 percent."

Hassan nodded. "Run your tests. You know where I am."

Anton took the brief case to the back room. Once inside he quickly locked the door.

"Well done, Anton," said Benny Machaim of the Mossad. He turned to his executive officer, Moshe Eisen. "We have this bastard right where we want him.

Moshe took the case from Anton, placing it on the metal table they had already prepared. "Heavy sucker isn't it?" He opened it and dumped the bags on the table. Benny emptied all of the bags of legitimate diamonds into a diplomatic pouch.

Benny then placed a canvas bag on top of the metal table. "We simply refill the plastic bags with these fakes."

Moshe and Anton smirked. "They won't be buying weapons anytime soon with this worthless crap."

"And best of all," said Benny, "the Sheik is going to place the blame on Hassan for the theft."

Anton bid Benny and Moshe farewell as they left out the back door with the real diamonds. Anton then quickly arranged the fake diamonds back into their proper place in the briefcase. "Time for Act II to start," he said to himself as he looked in the mirror, straitened his tie, and brushed his hair back. Satisfied, he opened the door and proceeded back out to provide Hassan with the bad news.

Hasson had just finished his drink as Anton placed the briefcase down on the wooden table. "I hope you have a better price to offer me," said Hasson as he helped himself to yet another scotch.

Anton looked to the guard and nodded, signaling he may have a need for his services. "Well, after my initial look at what you have," he said, "I think we will pass."

Hassan looked dumfounded. "What do you mean, *pass*? We have to barter a little. Some back and forth action. Give me a number."

"These are low-grade industrial diamonds," Anton lied. "We have a reputation to uphold. We really don't deal in such, *such trash*."

"What?" said Hassan, a little tipsy after drinking three glasses of scotch. He stood up. "I will take my business down the street to your competitor." He was secretly hoping Anton would stop him. Thinking it was all part of the bargaining process.

"Please, be my guest," said Anton. He looked over to the guard. "Will you escort Hassan to the door?"

Hassan knew this was the only shop that would deal in stolen diamonds. It was here or nowhere. "Give me a number," said Hassan in desperation as the guard now held him by his arm as he pulled him towards the door. "I'll take ten percent!"

"I'm sorry, sir," said Anton. "But as I stated, we do not deal in such low quality diamonds."

The guard slid the bolts on the door into the open position and gingerly eased Hassan outside onto the sidewalk.

Hassan stood on the busy sidewalk clutching his case with both arms for a minute or two wondering if he should approach another shop. He had to convert them to cash so he could give half to the Sheik and use the other half to escape to the islands somewhere.

He started walking south on Talstrasse. After passing several well-appointed shops, he stopped to look in an elegant window advertising a sale on gold and diamond jewelry. He was about to enter when a men and a woman in regal attire approached him.

"Excuse me, sir" said the stylishly dressed woman. "Do you know the way to Cofferdame Strasse?"

Hassan was about to answer when the man pulled a long, thin stiletto from his sleeve and shoved it into Hassan's heart, killing him instantly. The man and woman each took an arm and placed Hassan on a nearby bench, the hat on his head now pulled down over his face as if he were sleeping. They took his suitcase and blended into the crowd.

A block away Benny and Moshe watched as the event played out. Satisfied DoDo and Rachel had indeed eliminated their target they shook hands in congratulations and continued on to their embassy.

"We have done a good thing," said Moshe. "Now you can retire, my friend."

Benny nodded. *"Yes, now I can retire."*

CHAPTER 54

Florida Keys

The sun had just set an hour ago as Jim and Nora sat lounging on the stern of the *Irish Rebel* drinking a glass of Bordeaux. "So is this how I am supposed to spend the rest of my life with you, Mr. Dieter?" said Nora. "Drinking wine and traveling the world, getting kidnapped, and shot at?"

"Only if you play your cards right, Mrs. Dieter," he replied. "I'll try and keep the getting shot at and kidnapped part to a minimum."

"Oh, I bet you will."

Eian and Shannon boarded just as Nora finished.

"How was your swim?" she asked.

Shannon smiled. "The ocean is like bathwater down here," she replied. "I could definitely live here for a few months out of the year."

"You wouldn't miss your sheep?" cracked Eian.

"Are you kidding, this is my first vacation in three years. The sheep are in good hands."

Eian nodded his thanks to Jim for the two glasses of wine he offered, handing one to Shannon.

"I still can't believe my father left me all of those diamonds," said Shannon. "I still think what happened to us was a dream. I mean between the diamonds and Hassan kidnapping us."

Jim motioned for them to sit down and join them.

After a few minutes of silence Jim spoke. "While you guys were having a nice swim, the Brits and the Israelis provided me with a little more intel on the Amber Room theft if you think you can handle it?" He held up a recently delivered Fed Express envelope.

"As long as it doesn't involve us going after long lost treasure," he replied. "I'm done. I have enough money to keep me until dooms day."

Everyone laughed at Eian's response.

"No more treasure talk," said Jim. "Scouts honor."

Eian held up his glass. "All right my man, you may provide us with the details."

"You are going to love this," Jim said as he topped off Nora's glass, then his own. He removed documents from the Fed Express envelope, documents that he and

Nora had already read. "Perluci, that tricky bastard didn't really steal, per se, the Amber Room from Dr. Rohde in Konigsburg. The two of them had a double switch on."

"You're kidding me?" shot back Eian. "I knew he was a crook lad when I first laid eyes on him."

Nora held up her hand. "Here him out. Its gets even more interesting."

Jim continued. "Rohde knew the war was coming to a close and he was going to be on the losing side. Perluci restated the Vatican offer to him and his wife of $1million US in gold and free passage out of Prussia for the Amber Room. Think about it. Do you remember Dr. Rohde in the basement of the church? He had one of his soldiers open a crate to verify its contents? It was all for show. He wanted the soldiers as witnesses that the crates actually contained pieces of the Amber Room. Who would suspect that the rest of the wooden crates would be empty? Then Dr. Rohde had them moved back to the castle and the gallery where they were originally stored. At the time, the gallery and the church were the only parts of the castle left untouched by the bombing raids. The burgermiester, or mayor of the city, along with everyone else in civilian authority thought the bombing raids would cease since the city was mostly destroyed. But they were wrong. The final British bombing raid in August destroyed what remained of Konigsburg castle and with it, the Amber Rooms bottom panels. Remember, Perluci had the top panels and Rohde the bottom. Perluci knew he couldn't have a convoy of three trucks take the whole Amber room through enemy territory back to the Vatican so he chose only the more valuable of the panels; the bejeweled top panels. Hence only needing one truck. Of course, Dr. Rohde knew the raids would continue until the end of the war. At least that is what he had hoped. It's the only way he and his wife could escape the clutches of both the Gestapo and the Soviet KGB. As Rohde walked amongst the ruins of Königsberg castle on that fateful August day, he observed the area where the crates were stored had been completely consumed by fire. Nothing left but the overwhelming scent of amber resin from the bottom panels that hung in the air. A slight smile must have escaped his lips since when he realized he was $1M dollars in gold richer. Perluci had informed him that the Amber Room Bottom panels had to be destroyed for him to collect his money. I'm sure if the bombing raid didn't destroy the crates Rohde would have staged a fire or something along those lines to destroy the evidence. Perluci also told Dr. Rohde that he and his wife had to stay in Konigsburg until after the Russian troops arrived. They had to explain what happened to their Amber Room. Show them where the crates where stored. It lent some credibility to his story when the Russians interrogated the German soldiers who helped move the Amber Room crates from the church. They unwittingly helped to corroborate his story."

"Then with Dr. Rodhe and his wife faking their own deaths, remember, they found no bodies, they were able to use the Vatican Passports Perluci provided, escape to the west and collect the $1M in gold he had promised them."

"So Perluci, with Dr. Rohde's assistance, was able to dupe not only the Russians and the Nazis but also the Vatican. The bottom panels were destroyed in Königsberg and the Vatican had one crate of Amber Room top panels, the rest being worthless junk. And Perluci kept the rest of the Amber Room's top panels hidden in a series of graves in Northern Italy all of these years."

Eian looked to Nora, and then Jim, each of them smiling at each other. "So for 80 plus years the Vatican thought they had the Amber Room in their Vatican Vaults but what they really had was a bunch of worthless junk?"

Perluci was a sneaky bastard.

CHAPTER 55

Present Day, St Petersburg (formally Leningrad) Russia

Andrei Popov stood admiring the Amber Rooms top panels installation. It had been a very long time since he had viewed the original Amber Room panels together. Exactly 78 years to be precise. He remembered the day as if it were only yesterday. Standing beside his father, Anatoly Popov, the Director of the Palace as the German Army stood at the gates of the museum. It was little Andrei who had originally proposed the idea of hiding the panels behind wallpaper due to the Russian curators inability to move the panels.

He still carried some sense of guilt all of these years thinking it was he who allowed the panels to be found.

His father would be proud of him if he were still alive. To see the original panels occupying their rightful spot in the Catherine Palace. At least they weren't destroyed as so many *experts* had originally thought.

His new friends, Jim and Nora Dieter, stood beside him in lieu of his father. They were just as worthy as family since returning the Amber Rooms top panels to the Russian government for reinstallation onto the Catherine Palaces walls. Of course, the $5 million euro reward they received had done nothing to discourage them.

Jim and Nora had recently relayed the arduous journey the panels had undertaken since their theft by German soldiers during the war. From the German Army theft, to Dr. Rohde's theft, to Perluci pilfering it from everyone and burying his prize in an Italian graveyard. The story brought a tear to his eye thinking of the many who had died for the panels. Moreover, the humor he found in the thought of everyone thinking they knew what happened to the original Amber Room.

A workman called Andrei over to inspect one of the panels, pointing to some deep cuts. "These look very serious, sir," said the workman. "They will have to be repaired."

Andrei pulled a jewelers magnification piece from his pocket. After several minutes he motioned Jim and Nora over. He handed the Jewelers piece to Jim. "What do you think it is?" he said, pointing to a series of marks in the bottom corner. Jim adjusted the piece and studied the marks. "You have got to be kidding me?" he said before he then handed the piece to Nora for her inspection. "He wouldn't have," she responded.

In the bottom corner of the most bejeweled piece, Perluci had scratched his full name for all eternity: *Property of Antonio Perluci.*

THE END

Amazon Best Selling author Francis Joseph Smith has traveled to most of the world during his tenure in the Armed Forces (Navy & Air Force) and as an Analyst for an unnamed Government Agency, providing him with numerous fictional plot lines and settings for future use. His experiences provide readers with well researched, fast-paced action. Smith's novels are the result of years of preparation to become a fiction writer in the genre of Baldacci, Clancy, Flynn, Ludlum, Brown, Higgins, and Cussler.

Smith lives with his family in a small town outside of Philadelphia where he is currently in-work on his next novel.

.

Made in the USA
Monee, IL
26 November 2020

.49674709R00163